Loves and Hours

by Stephen Metcalfe

A SAMUEL FRENCH ACTING EDITION

SAMUEL FRENCH

FOUNDED 1830

NEW YORK HOLLYWOOD LONDON TORONTO

SAMUELFRENCH.COM

ISBN 978-0-573-69699-2   Printed in U.S.A.   #29115

MUSIC USE NOTE

IMPORTANT BILLING AND CREDIT
REQUIREMENTS

LOVES AND HOURS premiered at the Old Globe Theatre on March 23, 2003. The production was directed by Jack O'Brien, with the following cast and creative team:

DAN TILNEY . . . . .Brian Kerwin
HAROLD SCHWABB . . . . David Manis
ANDREA . . . . Nanka Sturgisy
DAN, JR. . . . . Brian Ibsen
SARA HOUGHTON. . . . . .Amanda Naughton
TOM HOUGHTON . . . . .Tom Tammi
LINDA . . . . Nance Williamson
REBECCA TILNEY . . . . Emmelyn Thayer
ANNE TRIPPLEHORN . . . . Monique Fowler
CHARLOTTE WALKER . . . . .Bridget Flanery

Scenic and Costume Design – Robert Morgan
Lighting Design – David F. Segal
Stage Manager – D. Adams
Assistant Stage Manager – Tracy Skoczelas
Set Design – Heather Cohn
Sound Design – Paul Peterson
Music – Bob James
Projection Design – Sage Marie Carter

CHARACTERS

Dan Tilney
Harold Schwab
Andrea
Dan, Jr.
Sara Houghton
Tom Houghton
Linda
Rebecca Tilney
Anne Tripplehorn
Charlotte Walker

(The sound of an organ playing. The light suggests sunlight through stained glass windows. Lights up on **DANIEL TILNEY**, *around 50, in a morning suit.)*

DAN. Like a lot of people, the only time I ever set foot in a church anymore is for a wedding. Beautiful day for one, isn't it? One of those old, white steepled churches on a town green. Guests disembark from expensive cars. Hands are shaken, cheeks are kissed. Children are playing near the fountain. Their parents coax them towards the church steps. Inside the doors, the registry is signed.

(lights up on:)

An altar boy lights a candle. A handsome, young groomsman escorts an elderly woman down the isle. The minister adjusts his vestments. The photographer checks his lenses. The church is full now. People wave at one another, fanning themselves, chatting quietly. And suddenly:

(Bridal fanfare beings. The veiled bride enters. The groom, **HAROLD SCHWABB**, *also around 50, enters. They face one another.)*

MINISTER. *(actor played by* **TOM HOUGHTON***)* In sickness and in health. To love and to cherish. Till death do us part.

(to **DAN***)*

Do you have the ring?

DAN. Oh. Sorry.

(to the audience)

I'm the best man.

*(***HAROLD** *slips the ring on the bride's finger.)*

MINISTER. By the power vested in me, I pronounce you man and wife. You may kiss the bride.

(**HAROLD** *lifts the veil and kisses the bride. The Wedding March begins. And as bride and groom turn to face the audience, we see the bride's face. She is lovely. She is in her 20s.*)

DAN. All right, stop the music.

(*The Wedding March stops in mid-note.* **HAROLD** *and the bride,* **ANDREA,** *freeze in mid-smile*)

What's wrong with this picture? Clothes, fine. Wedding gown, very nice. See it yet? I'm sure you do. My best friend, Harold Schwabb, is 49 years old. His blushing bride, Andrea, is 24. Need I say, she is young enough to be his daughter? Okay, let's go to the reception.

(*Lightchange. Upstage fills with people. They surround the bridal couple, drinking, chatting, congratulating.*)

Oh. And that handsome, young groomsmen?

(**DAN TILNEY JR.,** *20, moves downstage, to join a woman, late 40s.*)

That's my son, Dan Junior. And the woman he's talking to is Harold's sister, Julia.

(**DAN** *moves upstage.*)

DAN JR. Friend of the bride or groom?

JULIA. (*kissing his cheek*) Neither, darling, but somehow I got invited anyway.

DAN JR. I was looking for you at the church, Aunt Julia. I didn't see you.

JULIA. I've seen your Uncle Harold get married, darling; I didn't feel a need to do it again. (Hello!) Actually, I arrived late and watched from the back. When the minister got to the part about all my worldly goods, I thee endow, I thought the bridesmaids were all going to turn and do a cheer.

DAN JR. You know, I hear Uncle Harold is picking up the tab for all this?

JULIA. It's the new etiquette, Sweetheart. When a man marries a bimbo half his age, he pays for the privilege by picking up the tab.

(They move upstage. Another couple moves downstage. **SARA HOUGHTON** *is a very attractive late 30s; her husband,* **TOM,** *the same. Both have smiles frozen on their faces.)*

SARA. Hi. Hello.

TOM. Hi. Nice to see you.

*(***TOM** *drains his glass of champagne. As a waitress passes, he puts his empty glass on the her tray and takes a full one.)*

DAN. *(to the audience)* Oh – that's Sara and Tom Houghton. They arrived late.

SARA. Are you planning on talking at all or are you just going to drink?

TOM. I'm talking.

SARA. Not to me. (Hello!)

TOM. You're the one pulling the silent treatment, Sara. (Hey, there!)

SARA. I told you, there'd be no parking close to the church.

TOM. I thought there'd be valet. Shoot me.

SARA. And sometimes wouldn't I'd like to. (Hi.)

TOM. And more often than not, you make that perfectly clear.

BOTH OF THEM. *(cheerfully; to different people)* Hi!

TOM. Well, if you'll excuse me, I'm going to go kiss the bride.

SARA. You already have.

TOM. I'm going to do it again.

SARA. Tom, I just thought it would have been nice if we could've –

(but he's gone)

…sat together in the church.

(A moment. She turns, glass in hand and walks right into –)

DAN JR. Whoops –

SARA. Oh, I am so sorry.

DAN JR. My fault.

SARA. Hardly. Oh, look what I've done. Thank goodness it wasn't full.

(She wipes at his jacket with her napkin.)

DAN JR. No problem, it's rented. How you doing' Mrs. Houghton.

(off her confused look)

Dan Tilney? Dan and Linda Tilney are my parents?

SARA. Dan? Little Dan? Who used to live down the block?

DAN JR. Yeah.

SARA. Oh, my God. It's been, what, five or six years at least.

DAN JR. More like ten.

SARA. Look at you, you're all grown up, you're huge, you're –

(really looking at him)

…you're really beautiful.

(embarrassed)

And it is such a surprise to see you here. What have you been up to?

DAN JR. Well –

*(Chatting, they move away. **DAN** moves downstage.)*

DAN. *(calling back)* Yeah, we'll do that! Good, looking forward to it! You too!

(then; to the audience)

God. I have no idea who I was just talking to. I hate weddings. You're always running into people. They ask you questions you don't feel like answering. How you been? How you doing? Then they tell you how they're doing. And you have to listen and smile and pretend you're interested. It's exhausting.

(A woman, 40s, approaches.)

LINDA. Don't tell me, you're wondering how long you have to stay till you can go home.

(DAN turns in surprise.)

DAN. Linda, what are you doing here? (This is my wife, Linda).

LINDA. What, just because we're divorced, I don't get invited to an old friend's wedding?

DAN. (Ex-wife.) Harold said you weren't coming.

LINDA. *(teasing him)* Was it Harold who invited me? I've been telling everyone you did.

(and then, seriously:)

Relax, I just wanted to see Rebecca.

(A young woman, mid-20s, comes through the crowd, sees them. LINDA turns hopefully.)

DAN. (Our daughter, Rebecca.)

(REBECCA quickly turns away.)

I'm sorry.

LINDA. When do you think she's going to stop blaming me, Dan? All the diapers I cleaned, all the boo-boos I bandaged. I take up with a perfectly lovely lawyer and suddenly she won't talk to me.

DAN. I don't think it's Janet's profession that has her bent out shape.

LINDA. And I thought we raised our children to be open minded.

DAN. How is Janet?

LINDA. Fine. We're buying a townhouse.

DAN. Her kids talking to her?

LINDA. Oh, now don't you get bitter on me. What about you. Seeing anyone yet?

DAN. No.

LINDA. The child bride doesn't have any friends?

DAN. I haven't asked.

LINDA. Well…you're passably attractive, relatively prosperous, no deviant personality traits that I know of. Once you put your mind to it, I'm sure you'll be getting laid on a regular basis.

DAN. Linda, there's only been one time in my life I ever got "laid" on a regular basis.

LINDA. Really? When was that?

DAN. When I met you.

(A fond moment between them.)

I'll talk to Rebecca.

LINDA. Thanks. I'll call.

(She moves away.)

DAN. Did mention that I hate weddings? That's not true. I hate social gatherings of any kind.

(He turns away. **DAN JR.** *and* **SARA** *circle back.)*

DAN JR. Mom and Dad got divorced about a year ago. Mom decided she was a lesbian.

SARA. *(almost choking on her drink)* That must of come as a bit of a shock to your Dad.

DAN JR. I guess. He's okay now. He and I are still in the house over on Mercer Street. Rebecca's up in L.A. She's started her internship at UCLA Medical Center. Pediatrics.

SARA. So you, you must be…

DAN JR. I'm a Junior at Georgetown in the fall.

SARA. Georgetown.

DAN JR. Yeah. A transfer. I did the last two years out at State – which was great but – I figured it was time for a change. Or at least time for me to stop living at home. You still a stockbroker?

SARA. Good memory. Yes. Yes, I am.

*(***TOM HOUGHTON*** *enters. He's on his cell phone, laughing with someone.)*

TOM. Good, we'll do that, good! Good, you get us the tee time!

(reacting to something said)

Hah! You dog!

(disconnecting; then:)

Sara. Where you been? I've been looking all over for you.

SARA. I've been right here.

*(**DAN JR.** thrusts out a hand.)*

DAN JR. How you doing', Mr. Houghton. Dan Tilney.

TOM. Huh?

SARA. Dan and Linda's son.

TOM. Oh, right, yeah. Dan. Look at you, all grown up.

SARA. Dan was just telling me he's working for a contractor this summer.

TOM. Oh, yeah?

DAN JR. My Dad says it'll help me appreciate money to work at something where I don't make any.

TOM. He's full of it but don't tell him I said so.

*(to **SARA**)*

Don't wander off again. We're out of here soon.

SARA. We just got here.

TOM. The golf's on TV at three.

SARA. Oh. Of course.

TOM. Oh, and I'm on a plane to New York tomorrow. Nice to see you, Dan.

*(to **SARA**)*

Be where I can find you.

*(He strides away. **SARA** looks away, embarrassed. Music begins. Upstage, people break into couples and begin to dance.)*

DAN JR. Hey, Mrs. Houghton, how about dancing with me?

SARA. Oh…I don't think so….

DAN JR. Come on, it's one of the responsibilities of the groomsmen, to make sure all the women at the wedding dance at least one dance.

SARA. No, it's not. But it should be. All right.

(**DAN JR.** *offers his arm. She takes it. They join the dancing couples.* **DAN** *circling back, surprised, watching them go.* **HAROLD** *now joining him.*)

HAROLD. Hey, how you doin', buddy!

DAN. Huh? Oh, fine. Hey, is that Sara Houghton?

HAROLD. Huh? Yeah, I'm doing some venture capital stuff with Tom. Still some miles left on that chassis, huh?

DAN. We were neighbors. Dan saw her in a bikini one day. It was like seeing Everest for the first time.

(**DAN** *and* **HAROLD** *watch the couples swirl and dance. The bride dances with* **TOM HOUGHTON**.)

HAROLD. Look at her, Dan. Just looking at her is a religious experience. She should be bronzed like a work of art. She's keeping me young, I'm doing things. I'm screwing more than you can believe. We have gotta find one for you, buddy.

DAN. Thanks but I'll pass.

(*The couples dance offstage.*)

HAROLD. Okay, come here. Come on, I want to ask you something. You're walking down the street, you pass a woman, she thinks what when she sees you?

DAN. A woman? I don't think she thinks anything.

HAROLD. Exactly. And you know why she doesn't?

DAN. Do I want to?

HAROLD. You've lost the warrior within, Buddy-boy.

DAN. Warrior.

HAROLD. The one within. The one that's in every man. The hunter, the fighter, the lover. Huh?

DAN. You've been going to those weekend men's group gatherings again, haven't you, Harold?

HAROLD. Your warrior needs to learn how to express himself again, Dan. He needs to ripple and flex. He needs to bang a drum.

(He throws himself down and does several push-ups.)

Do you think I would have gotten anywhere with Andrea if I hadn't been working out with a personal trainer three times a week?

(rising)

I still am. I'm biking, jogging. Not only that, Andrea now has me on a vegetarian diet supplemented by 17 different vitamins and minerals a day.

DAN. That's a lot.

HAROLD. That's nothing. Two days a week I do yoga.

(He does a convoluted yoga pose.)

I do a hundred crunches every night before I go to bed. I drink 12 glasses of distilled water.

DAN. I'd imagine you're up at night peeing a lot.

HAROLD. *(painful coming out of his pose)* I'm serious, Dan. My personal trainer. Three times a week and you'll feel good, you'll look good. Chicks will dig you again.

DAN. "Chicks," huh?

HAROLD. Julia will explain.

DAN. *(turning; apprehensive)* Julia?

(JULIA has entered.)

JULIA. Harold and I have been talking, Dan. We both agree.

DAN. That's a first.

JULIA. It's time for you to start dating again. You don't go out, you don't socialize. We're worried about you.

DAN. I'm touched.

JULIA. I am too. Now. I have someone I want you to meet. She is smart, funny and successful. She's also recently divorced.

HAROLD. Julia thought it'd be nice if you had one thing in common.

JULIA. Do I detect sarcasm, Harold?

HAROLD. My sister and I agree you should date, we don't agree on who. Julia, Dan doesn't need you to set him up with dates.

DAN. Thanks, Harold.

HAROLD. He has me to do that.

JULIA. Oh, please. Unlike some people, Dan doesn't want to end up dating some taxi dancer from Pamona.

HAROLD. Excuse me, are you referring to Andrea?

JULIA. Why would you ever think that?

HAROLD. Admit it, Julia, finally admit it – you don't like her.

JULIA. Like is such a strong word.

HAROLD. Funny, Julia. Real funny. You listen to her, Dan, you'll end up with some neurotic 50 year old with a chip on her shoulder.

JULIA. And if he listens to you, he'll end up with some stripper with hair extensions and a silicone brain.

HAROLD. *(to DAN)* You got a problem with that?

DAN. All right, both of you, stop. Maybe I can make this easy for you. I don't need anyone to set me up with anyone. I can do it myself.

(They snicker and laugh.)

JULIA. Dan, please.

HAROLD. We're trying to be serious here, Bud.

JULIA. You're good with animals, not people. It's why you're a veterinarian.

HAROLD. Yeah. People you gotta talk to.

DAN. Wait. What. I talk. I talk all the time. I'm talking right now and I'm saying I'm not interested. Who around here doesn't understand simple English?

(The bride, ANDREA suddenly enters.)

ANDREA. There you are!

HAROLD. *(to JULIA)* Don't you say a word.

(to ANDREA)

Hey, honey-baby!

ANDREA. Oh. I should have known you'd be out here with the people you love. And now I love them too.

(She stumbles slightly. **DAN** *catches and steadies her.)*

HAROLD. Whoops! I think someone's had a little too much champagne.

ANDREA. I love you, Dan. I love you because Harold loves you. I love you too, Julia. Even though Harold speaks badly of you, I love you very much.

(then:)

Oh, Julia, I wish you could have seen the look on your face when I was stuffing cake in Harold's mouth.

JULIA. Stuffing something down Harold's throat. How I envied you.

ANDREA. Ohh, Miss Grumpy Face! Don't worry. You still might get married some day. There's hope! Harold, we should go in. The helicopter's picking us up out in front in 20 minutes.

HAROLD. Lead the way, honey-baby. I love you guys. Be good.

ANDREA. See you in two weeks!

HAROLD. We'll continue this when I get back! Wish me luck!

*(***HAROLD*** *and* ***ANDREA*** *exit.)*

JULIA. A helicopter?

DAN. Andrea wanted to leave the wedding in a helicopter.

JULIA. Please. It's Andr-ay-a.

DAN. How come you never got married, Julia?

JULIA. …Would you believe the only man I ever loved, married someone else before I could tell him how I felt about him?

DAN. No.

JULIA. Why not?

DAN. Because, Julia, you've never met anyone in your entire life, you didn't immediately tell them exactly how you felt about them.

*(**REBECCA** suddenly enters. She looks disraught.)*

DAN. *(cont.)* Hi, Beck, what's that?

REBECCA. *(holding out:)* It's – I – I caught the wedding bouquet!

(Bursting into tears, she runs off.)

JULIA. I'll be in touch.

*(She exits. **DAN** looks up as we hear the sound of a helicopter rising.)*

DAN. Believe me, it was a bitch to tie tin cans on.

(a sigh)

Weddings. I hate weddings.

*(Lightchange. **DAN** pulls off his tie.)*

I find weddings almost as disruptive as, well, children. Especially adult children who you can't tell what to do anymore. Well – you can but they won't listen. Actually they never listen. It's just that young children you can coerce with the threat of bodily harm.

*(**REBECCA** enters. She has a bag over her shoulder.)*

REBECCA. Daddy, will you stop!?

DAN. Aw, come on, honey, your room's ready, you can get a good night sleep, go back up tomorrow.

REBECCA. It's not "my room," Daddy. I don't live here anymore. And I have rounds tomorrow, I want to get back tonight.

DAN. At least have a cup of coffee.

REBECCA. Daddy, I know what you want to talk about and I don't want to. You have to let Mom and me work it out ourselves.

DAN. It's not just your Mom, Beck…you seem unhappy lately. Like you're keeping everything inside.

REBECCA. Daddy, you know what I deal with everyday? Sick children. I have a lot on my mind. Now I have to go. I love you.

(She exits. **DAN** *sighs. He takes off his jacket and tie.)*

DAN. She was always the perfect kid. By the time she was in the sixth grade, she had her entire life planned. She got through college in three years. Med school in two.

*(***DAN JR.*** *enters. He is brushing his teeth with one hand and eating a sandwich with the other.)*

DAN. Where as with this kid. Well, I rest my case.

DAN JR. Dad? Hey, Dad?

DAN. Yeah, Dan, what is it?

DAN JR. I was talking to Mom at the wedding? She was saying maybe I could start spending a little more time with her, you know, weekends and stuff, now that they'll have a bedroom for me now and everything.

DAN. Oh. Well, how do you feel about that?

DAN JR. Well…I head back East in a couple of months. Who knows when I'll be back or how much I'll be seeing you guys or anything. Maybe I should spend a little time with Mom while I can, you know? I think maybe she kinda needs it That is, if you don't mind.

DAN. No. No, I think it's a good idea.

(He hands his jacket and tie to **DAN JR.***)*

DAN JR. I will then. Thanks, Dad.

DAN. No problem.

*(***DAN JR.*** *exits.)*

And to think there was a time I wondered if I'd ever get my life back. You raise your children to leave you and then you have no idea what you're going to do with yourself when they're gone. You wonder how it came to this. You wonder, how it is, you ever found yourself here. You wonder.

*(***DAN*** *exits. Lightchange.* **DAN JR.** *leads a dog out onto the stage. The dog has a lampshade on its head.* **JULIA** *enters from the other side of the stage.)*

DAN JR. Hey, Aunt Julia, what are you doing here?

JULIA. I was about to ask you the same thing.

DAN JR. Dad's kennel assistant is on vacation and his secretary called in sick. I'm filling in.

JULIA. And this is?

DAN JR. This is retired Admiral "Biff" Mackey's dog, Gus.

JULIA. I know the Mackeys. What's the problem?

DAN JR. Swollen testicles. He's really proud of them and likes to show them off in front of Mrs. Mackey's bridge club.

JULIA. And the dog?

DAN JR. The dog has fleas.

 (handing over a clipboard:)

 Listen, I was just taking Gus for a walk. This is Dad's schedule. Bring him up to date, huh?

JULIA. But –

DAN JR. Thanks, Aunt Julia!

 (He exits. **JULIA** *begins to peruse the clipboard,* **DAN** *enters. in a white lab coat.)*

DAN. Julia, what do you think you're doing?

JULIA. Being nosy.

DAN. Where's Dan?

JULIA. A dog took him for a walk. Now pay attention. You've got a heartworm patient in A, a dog that swallowed his tennis ball in B and a cat in C that's scheduled to have his teeth cleaned. Oooh – and your accountant called.

DAN. Ex-accountant.

JULIA. You're scheduled to meet with the IRS people next Monday. You didn't tell me you were being audited.

DAN. For good reason.

 (taking the clipboard)

 Now unless you want to help me clean the cat's teeth in C, I'm busy.

JULIA. All right, now listen –

DAN. I'm *busy*, Julia.

JULIA. I've made reservations for two, Saturday night at Cicero's at 7:30 in your name and I want no guff.

DAN. Julia, I thought we weren't going to do this.

JULIA. Who said anything about we? You can pick Anne up at her home which isn't too far from yours –

DAN. Oh, is that her name? "Anne"?

JULIA. – quiet! – or you can meet her at the restaurant, your choice.

DAN. Thank you for leaving me one.

JULIA. Oh, stop it, Dan. We're not talking about falling in love. We're talking about some company, we're talking about getting out of the house and going somewhere other than the office. Fighting the loneliness, that's all.

DAN. You don't.

JULIA. You need someone, Dan. You always have. I don't.

DAN. All right. Tell "Anne" I'll pick her up.

JULIA. I already have. And you're welcome.

DAN. I didn't say thanks.

JULIA. You will.

(She exits. Lightchange. **DAN** *takes off his lab coat. He's wearing a sports jacket underneath.)*

DAN. And so, the following Friday night, with Dan Jr. off to visit his mother, I found myself walking up to a strange house in a strange neighborhood in a strange city in a strange country on a strange planet accompanied by my stomach which was strangely sick with nerves.

(A doorbell. Ding-dong! **JULIA** *immediately enters.)*

JULIA. *(pleasantly)* Hell-o.

(For a moment, **DAN** *thinks he's come to the wrong house.)*

DAN. *(entering)* Julia? What are you doing here.

JULIA. We're having a crisis of confidence, I'm afraid.

*(*ANNE *– the actress playing* **LINDA** *– enters. She takes one look at* **DAN** *and turns and exits, putting her hand over her mouth so she won't vomit.)*

JULIA. *(cont.)* Anne is no longer sure she wants to go.

DAN. Oh? Too bad.

JULIA. Don't worry. She will if I tag along.

DAN. Julia…

JULIA. I'll just help break the ice and then find a good time to duck out, all right?

DAN. Julia – there's not going to be a good time. I don't want to do this.

JULIA. Don't be silly. You'll both get to know each other, it'll be fine.

ANNE. *(entering)* I'm ready.

> (**ANNE** *is now wearing a heavy raincoat, buttoned and belted like body armor and is clutching a umbrella.*)

JULIA. Annie, darling, you seem to be dressed for a hurricane.

ANNE. The Weather Channel said something about a front.

JULIA. A front.

> (*to* **DAN**)

Did you happen to notice a front?

DAN. Uh – no. All clear. No front.

ANNE. Oh. Well, I guess I don't need all this then, do I.

JULIA. I think not.

> (**ANNE** *takes off the raincoat. However, she neglects to put down the umbrella first and it becomes tangled. In a series of ungainly and finally violent movements, she frees herself of coat and umbrella. She smiles weakly.*)

ANNE. It's all right. I'm fine! We should just – go.

JULIA. Why don't we? I'll meet you both at the restaurant.

ANNE. No! I mean – we can all go in one car. Can't we?

JULIA. All right. I'll grab a cab when we get to the restaurant

DAN. *(aside)* Don't you dare.

> (*Lightchange. The three of them move to stand together as if in "a car";* **JULIA** *and* **DAN** *in the front;* **JULIA** *in the middle behind.*)

JULIA. Well! We're off! And Bon Voyage, I say!

(silence)

Any trouble finding the place, Dan?

DAN. No. Good directions.

(silence)

JULIA. Actually Dan doesn't live too far away.

ANNE. Really?

JULIA. He's over on Mercer.

(a beat)

You two are practically neighbors.

(a beat)

Actually I'm surprised you've never met.

(a beat)

Well. Now you have.

DAN. *(to the audience)* There was no way it could get worse.

(Sound of a siren. A police car's red and yellow light revolves behind them. They all stand, half smiles frozen on their faces. Finally:)

ANNE. I really should have warned you about that stop sign. No one ever sees it.

JULIA. Don't be silly, darling. Dan should have pulled over before we tried to help look for your contact.

*(**ANNE** rubs at one eye which is blinking and tearing.)*

ANNE. I wonder what's taking him so long.

DAN. Probably checking out my criminal record.

ANNE. Oh. Do you have one?

JULIA. I think Dan was joking, darling.

ANNE. Oh. Of course.

*(A semi-hysterical giggle, quickly stifled. Silence. **JULIA** finally glancing back at **ANNE** – say something.)*

ANNE. Uhm – Dan? Julia says you're a vegetarian.

DAN. What? No.

ANNE. What? But – Julia –

JULIA. What I said, darling, is that Dan's a veterinarian.

ANNE. Oh. Of course – you're a – veterinarian.

DAN. Yes. Yes, I am.

ANNE. That's lovely. I – I love animals.

DAN. Have any pets?

ANNE. No, no. I should, but –

JULIA. There are no shoulds, darling –

ANNE. No, but…we had a rabbit once. The one with the floppy ears?

DAN. A lop.

ANNE. Yes! And, well –

> *(giggling)*

> – it was sitting in the driveway one day, you know, just, well, sitting and my eldest daughter, she'd just gotten her driver's permit and she was practicing, and, well – she ran over the rabbit.

DAN. No.

ANNE. Yes! And the thing is, she was on the ride-around lawn mower at the time and –

JULIA. Oh, dear God.

ANNE. I know! It was terrible – bunny everywhere! – and – I don't know why I'm laughing – we were all very upset about it as you can imagine and…well, we decided not to get another pet for awhile, no. The rabbit was not a success.

DAN. *(to "the cop")* What's that? Sign where, here? Right.

> *(He mimes signing; then, annoyed:)*

> Yes, I will, officer, I will certainly try to keep my eyes open from now on, I'll certainly try to do that.

> *(with a hint of sarcasm)*

> No – thank *you*, officer. Goodbye.

ANNE. *(a beat)* He seemed nice.

(Lightchange. A bearded man in a dark suit, the **MAITRE'D** *[the actor playing* **HAROLD***] enters, holding menus.)*

DAN. Uh – excuse me – excuse me?

MAITRE'D. Yes. May I help you?

DAN. Yes – once again – we had a reservation.

MAITRE'D. And you are?

DAN. Tilney.

MAITRE'D. …Tilney, yes. Your table is not quite ready, perhaps if you would find a seat in the bar.

DAN. We have been waiting in the bar for 40 minutes. And there are no seats.

MAITRE'D. Yes, well, I'm afraid we're rather busy tonight, we –

(seeing her)

Ms. Schwabb Is it you?

JULIA. Hello, Antony.

MAITRE'D. Why, it's been ages. You're all together?

JULIA. Yes. Three, please.

MAITRE'D. Of course, yes…

(his seating chart)

That won't do…but that will do nicely.

(gathering menus; smiling)

Right this way, please.

(He waves a hand. A **WAITER** *[actor playing* **DAN JR.***] And waitress [the actress playing* **REBECCA***] bring on a table and chairs.)*

DAN. Been here before?

JULIA. Oh, now, don't get all huffy.

(They are seated. Handed menus.)

MAITRE'D. There we are. So very sorry to keep you waiting. And now, perhaps, something from the bar?

ANNE. Oh, I don't think so…

JULIA. Of course, you will. What's good for nerves, Antony?

MAITRE'D. For nerves, I recommend a double vodka martini with a twist, straight up, always.

JULIA. She'll have that. I will too.

DAN. Three.

(**ANTONY** *nods sagely and departs.*)

JULIA. Now then, let's have a wonderful dinner, shall we?

(*A middle aged man,* **ROGER,** *[the actor playing* **TOM HOUGHTON***], enters and approaches the table. He is accompanied by a young woman,* **SANDRA** *[the actress playing* **ANDREA***]).*)

ROGER. Anne?

ANNE. …Roger.

ROGER. (*gesturing off*) Sandra and just came in for some dinner and we saw you.

(*to* **DAN**)

Hello, there.

ANNE. I'm sorry. Roger, this is Dan and Julia. This is Roger.

ROGER. Dan. Julia. Sandra.

(*a moment*)

DAN. Would – you two like to join us?

ANNE. No!

ROGER. Thanks but we're meeting some people. They're over there.

(*He waves across stage.* **ANNE** *looks; then looks away.*)

Perhaps another time. Well. We'll let you get on with your evening. Just wanted to say hello. Good to see you getting out, Anne. You're looking great.

ANNE. Thank you. You too.

(**ROGER** *and* **SANDRA** *exit.*)

JULIA. Well. If I were you, Dan, I'd be jealous.

(*to* **ANNE**)

A friend?

ANNE. No.

JULIA. Neighbor?

ANNE. I'd move.

JULIA. Must be a relative then.

DAN. Pretty girl he's with.

ANNE. It's my ex-husband. And that couple he's joining are my ex-best friends.

JULIA. Oh, dear.

(The **WAITRESS** *puts drinks down on the table and departs.)*

DAN. We can go someplace else if you'd like

ANNE. No. We'll just run into someone else.

*(***ANNE** *drinks deep. She coughs.* **JULIA** *elbows* **DAN***.)*

DAN. Ow! Oh! Uh, so, Anne – where is it you know Julia from?

ANNE. We spin together.

DAN. …spin?

ANNE. The bike thing?

DAN. Oh! Right. The bike thing. For a moment I thought you meant the – flax into thread thing.

JULIA. *(laughing a little too hard)* Dan…funny.

ANNE. No. It's pathetic. This herd of middle aged women in leotards, pumping away on these silly bicycles, while some little health Nazi in a sweat band screams at us. Beating ourselves into shape. And for what? That? This?

(And suddenly **ANNE***'s face crumbles and she puts her head down on the table and weeps into her hands.* **DAN** *stares. No idea what to say. People are looking.)*

JULIA. Anne, darling, are you all right?

(She nods.)

JULIA. You don't seem all right.

(She shakes her head. The **WAITER** *approaches. With a bottle of wine.)*

WAITER. Good evening. The gentleman at the far table sends this over with his compliments.

(An anguished sob breaks from **ANNE**. *Rising, she hurries out of the room.)*

JULIA. *(glancing at the bottle label)* She did everything right, Dan. I know that for a fact. Everything. And it didn't make a difference. In the end he wanted something else.

(The wine)

Very cheap.

(Rising, she exits.)

DAN. *(calling after her)* I'll call!

(Lights down on **DAN**. *Lights up on* **SARA**. **TOM** *enters. He is in a bathrobe, drinking a beer.)*

SARA. Look at that moon.

TOM. You ever talk to the yard people about what's wrong with the lawn?

SARA. Mmm, they asked if you turned off the sprinkler system the last time it rained.

TOM. Sure I did, so? Water costs money.

SARA. Yeah, well, they said the lawn's dying because you didn't turn it back on.

(a moment)

Tom, what would you think if we built a pergola here in the backyard? You know, wood beams, grapevines. Remember the one that was at that old farmhouse we rented in France? We used to sit out there and drink wine and talk and…remember?

What do you think?

TOM. I don't see why you should care about grapevines when you can't even remember to tell me when the water's turned off on the lawn.

(exiting)

I'm in New York this week.

(Lights down on **SARA** *as she exits. Lightchange.* **DAN** *enters. He is holding a cardboard box of loose papers. He looks around.)*

DAN. Local IRS office. Even the portraits on the wall look intimidating.

(The box)

Oh – these are my financial records. Oh, yeah, I'm ready for this.

*(***CHARLOTTE WALKER*** enters. She is early to mid twenties.)*

CHARLOTTE. Mr. Tilney? I'm Charlotte Walker.

DAN. Yes, how do you.

CHARLOTTE. I'm fine, thanks. If you'll sit down, we'll get you started.

(They cross and sit down on opposite sides of a desk, stage right.)

I take it your accountant's not with you?

DAN. The last I heard, my accountant moved to Mexico.

CHARLOTTE. The way he's messed up your tax return, it should be on permanent basis. Would you like some coffee?

DAN. No – thanks. My stomach's a little, uh…

CHARLOTTE. I understand. Getting audited is no fun.

DAN. Just between us, is the auditor a decent guy or is he some sadistic bastard who gets his kicks out of harassing people?

CHARLOTTE. Well, he's not a sadist. And he's not a guy. He's me.

DAN. Oh. I'm sorry, I thought…

CHARLOTTE. It's all right. That's what people usually think. Do you have your financial records with you?

DAN. Yes, yes, I do

(He puts the box on the desk.)

CHARLOTTE. You *are* organized.

DAN. My wife used to handle all this. We were divorced last year.

CHARLOTTE. Oh. I'm sorry. Well. What we're going to do is go through your records and your return which I have right here. I'll be asking you some questions. Answer them as best you can and any questions that you have, please don't hesitate to ask me.

DAN. I won't.

CHARLOTTE. Good.

(She begins to read. **DAN** *watches her. She glances up. She smiles. And she goes back to work. Lights down on them and up on:)*

*(***SARA*** *enters. She is carrying supermarket bags.)*

DAN JR. Mrs. Houghton!

*(***DAN JR.*** *Enters. He is wearing a sleeveless t-shirt, jeans and workboots.)*

Mrs. Houghton, hey! It's me, Dan Tilney!

SARA. Well, of course it is. Dan. Hi. Hi.

DAN JR. I saw you from across the lot over there. How you doing?

SARA. I'm fine, I'm – what are you doing here?

DAN JR. Me and some of the guys on the crew are just hitting the Subway for lunch.

SARA. Oh. Me too. I mean – my lunch canceled and I'm catching up on some grocery shopping.

DAN JR. Cool.

SARA. You're all sweaty.

DAN JR. Yeah, well, you know, we've been working.

SARA. In the sun, obviously, because, well, you have a very nice tan.

DAN JR. You want some help?

SARA. Oh – no. My car's just over here.

DAN JR. Sara H.

SARA. What?

DAN JR. Your license plate. S A R A – H.

SARA. Oh. Right – it's embarrassing – it was a birthday gift from Tom.

DAN JR. The car?

SARA. No, the plate, just the…(plate). You have good eyes.

DAN JR. Yeah, well, you know, youth. Everything works.

SARA. Yes. Well. It's nice to see you again, Dan.

DAN JR. Yeah, you too.

(He starts to exit.)

SARA. Wait! Dan. Uh – I wondered if I could…ask your advice on something.

DAN JR. Yeah, sure.

SARA. I mean, not so much advice as…there's some work, we were thinking, Tom and I, of having done around the house and we were wondering if you – your contractor, that is – had any hours…available.

DAN JR. How big a job we talking about?

SARA. Not big. A pergola. That's an arbor, sort of…

DAN JR. It's latticework for vines, right?

SARA. *(surprised)* Yes.

DAN JR. It's a little small for the kind of work we do, Mrs. Houghton.

SARA. Oh.

DAN JR. But I could do it. I mean, if you don't mind weekends.

SARA. Well, no. No, I mean, I'd have to check with Tom but –

DAN JR. You gonna be home Saturday morning?

SARA. Uh – I think so.

DAN JR. Why don't I come by, check it out.

SARA. Oh. Well, that'd be fine – for both Tom and me – just fine.

DAN JR. I'll see you Saturday then.

SARA. Saturday it is.

DAN JR. See ya.

SARA. Bye.

> *(He turns and exits. She watches him go. She waves. And then, catches herself, annoyed:)*

SARA. Oh, get a fucking grip.

> *(She turns and exits. Lights up on the desk.* **CHARLOTTE** *runs some final numbers through a calculator. Hits the return. She rips off the paper and hands it to* **DAN.** **DAN** *looks at it.)*

CHARLOTTE. Still breathing?

DAN. It's not as bad as I thought it'd be.

CHARLOTTE. Now you don't have to pay this all at once. We can put you on a schedule.

DAN. No, I'd prefer to get it out of the way.

CHARLOTTE. Must be nice. Ready for coffee now?

DAN. No…thanks. Actually if that's everything –

CHARLOTTE. It is.

DAN. I'll be going then.

> *(***DAN*** rises. She rises with him.)*

DAN. And – I'll take care of this right away.

CHARLOTTE. If you don't, I know where to find you.

DAN. …What? You do?

CHARLOTTE. We have your address. Also you're Rebecca Tilney's father.

DAN. You know Rebecca?

CHARLOTTE. We were on cheerleaders together. In high school.

DAN. You went to high school with Rebecca?

CHARLOTTE. I was a junior, she was a senior. I hear Rebecca's in med school.

DAN. Finishing, yeah.

CHARLOTTE. She was always smart.

DAN. As you can tell from my tax return, she doesn't get it from me. A year younger than Becky, that makes you – ?

CHARLOTTE. I'm 25.

DAN. That's…a nice age. Well –

CHARLOTTE. Hey, you want to grab some lunch?

DAN. Lunch?

CHARLOTTE. I don't have another appointment until two. We could grab a quick bite. And you could tell me all about…Rebecca. Unless you have to run.

DAN. No. No, I – uh – no. Lunch would be – great.

CHARLOTTE. Cool.

(She exits.)

DAN. *(to the audience)* What. I had to eat.

(lightchange)

DAN. At this little place down on the wharf, we ordered a fish sandwich, a crab roll, an order of onion rings… at least, Charlotte did. I had the diet tuna plate with the rye crisps on the side. With two ice teas, it was all of sixteen fifty. And then it became really cheap because –

CHARLOTTE. *(entering with ice tea)* This is on me. You're already out enough money today.

(They sit.)

DAN. So, tell me, uhm –

CHARLOTTE. What's a nice girl like me doing, working for the IRS?

DAN. Exactly that.

CHARLOTTE. I was an accounting major in college and they offered me a job. And the salary's good and the benefits are great. The only thing wrong is people treat you like you're the dentist.

DAN. Yeah, well, the dentist uses Novocaine. And what do when you're not, you know…

CHARLOTTE. Putting people away for twenty years?

DAN. You get asked this all the time, don't you.

CHARLOTTE. Constantly. I sing.

DAN. What?

CHARLOTTE. When I'm not putting people away. I sing. Some friends and I, we started a band. I like to tell people I got into accounting because I wanted something I could really count on. Music's what I really love.

DAN. That's great.

A VOICE. Number 27.

CHARLOTTE. That's us. See if you can find us a place to sit outside.

(She moves away. The sound of sea gulls.)

DAN. It was so easy! She did all of the talking. All I had to do was nod, smile and listen. We threw french fries to the gulls. I got ketchup on my shirt. She wiped it off with a napkin. Very sweet. We walked back up from the wharf together. It felt like one of those television commercial, where the girl has bouncy hair and whiter teeth. And she was with me!

*(**CHARLOTTE** re-enters. **DAN** moves to join her as:)*

CHARLOTTE. – See, one of the things that is so cool about music is the way it touches the listener. I mean, not so much on a lyrical level though lyrics can be a very profound thing but on an emotional, almost telepathic level. Some songs you don't even understand the words to but they still say everything to you, you know? They can shake you up, change your life – and you really should stop me before I hurt someone.

DAN. No, this has been – I've enjoyed it.

CHARLOTTE. You're funny.

DAN. You're late.

CHARLOTTE. This has been nice.

DAN. Yeah. Yeah, it has.

(a moment)

Well, listen, uh –

CHARLOTTE. You have any plans for Friday night?

DAN. What?

CHARLOTTE. The band and I are playing a set in Solana Beach Friday night and if you wanted to come, we could grab a drink or a bite to eat after.

DAN. Charlotte, are you asking me out?

CHARLOTTE. Well, it didn't look like you were going to and I really do have to get back upstairs. I mean, the downside is you'll have to hear me sing but…

DAN. No. I'd like very much to hear you sing.

CHARLOTTE. All right. Here's my home number. Call me. We'll work out the details.

*(She writes her number on his hand. **DAN** grins, amused, at the audience. And then **CHARLOTTE** quickly kisses his cheek, turns and exits. Surprised, **DAN** stands a moment, touching his cheek, lost in thought.)*

DAN. All right, I was as shocked as you are. I mean, I don't consider myself a bad looking guy but let's face it, I'm not – uhm – I don't know, fill in the blank. And to be honest, as much as I'd enjoyed my time with her, I hadn't really allowed myself to think of her in that way.

(then;)

Okay, so I'm full of it. She was gorgeous and personable and sexy and when she smiled at me I felt it all the way down to my – toes. And let's be honest, my toes hadn't shown interest in much of anything in quite some time.

(turning away; turning back)

Oh – I almost forgot.

*(An electronic bell goes off. **DAN** turns as if looking around. He sees something that intrigues him – a duck headed fire poker. He picks it up. Waves it like a sword. And –)*

JULIA. There are matching tongs.

*(**DAN** turns, embarrassed.)*

That is, if you're interested.

DAN. Uh, no, no...I was just – driving by. I haven't been in here in awhile.

JULIA. It hasn't changed much.

DAN. No. I also wanted to find out if your friend was okay... from the other night.

JULIA. She's terribly embarrassed but she's fine. You know, I think I owe you an apology.

DAN. Me – why?

JULIA. Because I don't really know Anne all that well – just that she was divorced and seemed nice – I probably jumped the gun. It's just that I want to see you happy, Dan.

*(**DAN** probably paying attention to something else as he says:)*

DAN. You know, Julia, I was pretty devastated when Linda left me.

JULIA. I know.

DAN. Not so much the leaving. I believe every individual has the right to pursue their own happiness. It's just – by leaving, she put me in this position where I didn't know what was going to replace what had been a given in my life – that I was a married man. And I think what I've been trying to do is pretend that nothing had really changed. That I was – still – married. Well, I'm not, am I. Things have changed.

JULIA. So I should keep trying to set you up?

DAN. No – Harold should.

JULIA. Oh, go away you.

DAN. Thanks, Julia.

JULIA. Thanks for stopping by.

(She exits as – lightchange.)

DAN. Imagine if you will, a perfect dawn. The sun is just beginning to peek over the horizon. The birds have begun their morning song. One of those rare mornings where your bed feels like a warm cocoon and another hour of sleep is just a blissful sigh away.

*(**HAROLD** enters and begins jogging in place. He's wears high tech jogging clothes, bug eyed sunglasses, a jogger's back-pack and a bizarre hat that looks like something out of the French Foreign Legion. Ding-dong!)*

DAN. *(cont.)* And then downstairs the doorbell rings and you're suddenly wide awake wondering who the hell has the nerve to bother you at –

(looking)

– Harold, it's six o'clock in the morning!

HAROLD. Rise and shine, rise and shine! I'm home from the honeymoon and I'm feeling so fine!

DAN. What are these things on your body?

HAROLD. This is an advanced ergonomic fluid distribution system, Dan. 64 ounces of energy sustaining glucose, amino acids and complex carbohydrates upon demand.

DAN. Wow, what's in it?

HAROLD. Hawaiian Punch.

DAN. And the hat?

HAROLD. Blocks out the sun's ultraviolet rays. The aging process especially around the neck and eyes is slowed down and in some cases reversed completely.

DAN. I doubt anyone's looking at your neck and eyes, Harold.

*(**HAROLD** begins to stretch.)*

HAROLD. So how'd the big date go?

DAN. Who said I went on a date?

HAROLD. Who set up the date?

DAN. What did you do, Harold, call your sister the minute you got home?

HAROLD. Who waited till we got home? So come on, how'd it go?

DAN. Her ex-husband sent over a very nice bottle of wine.

HAROLD. Hah! There, you see? That's why you need a younger woman, bud. They have no emotional baggage! They're a blank slate – raw clay waiting to be molded by the experienced artist.

DAN. As matter of fact, I have met a younger woman, Harold.

HAROLD. What? Where?

DAN. The internal revenue service. I was being audited.

HAROLD. Some people have all the luck. And did you ask her out?

DAN. As a matter of fact, she asked me.

HAROLD. Fuck you. You are kidding. Do you know what I had to do to get Andrea to go out with me?

DAN. As I remember, you offered to fly her first class to Maui.

HAROLD. That was the second date. The first date, I just promised to pay her rent.

DAN. And I'm sure it was worth it.

HAROLD. So when are you seeing this hot young chick?

DAN. I'm seeing this young lady tonight.

HAROLD. Ho-ho, you are not going jogging, buddy, you need to conserve your strength.

DAN. I was never going jogging, Harold. As soon as you leave, I'm going back to bed.

HAROLD. Okay, okay but listen. You're gonna date teenagers, buy some clothes that don't make you like a fifty year old.

DAN. I am a fifty year old.

HAROLD. Not after tonight you're not!

(exiting)

Call me when you get home!

DAN. And she's not a teenager!

(lightchange)

DAN. Actually I'm not quite fifty. It's fine line, I know, but one worth preserving. However! That night, with towel around my thickening waist, and Harold's words ringing in my ears, I found myself staring into the mirror. And what I saw did not inspire confidence.

(Music begins as –)

DAN. *(cont.)* I applied deodorant. It was the same deodorant I had used for thirty years. It now smelled of senility. I trimmed my nose and ear hair, which had sprouted like an Amazon rain forest in the course of the day.

*(We see images of **DAN** on the scrim behind as:)*

I combed my hair. I combed it forward. I combed it back. I parted it in the middle. Using my son's mousse, I tried a spike or two. I was not encouraged. I dressed in what I've come to think of as my uniform – khakis, loafers and button down collar shirt. It wasn't right. I put a sweater on over the shirt. Still no. I tried a sportsjacket over the sweater. It was getting worse. Wearing nothing but my underwear, I ventured down the hall into the wasteland that was my son's bedroom. Going straight to his closet, I found at my disposal –

(Quick flashes of athletic jerseys, baggy shorts and jeans, Sketchers, down vests, hooded sweatshirts, sneakers and assorted baseball caps.)

– not only a veritable garbage dump of things no one in their right mind would ever wear, but also an old issue of Playboy and what appeared to be the remains of a month old peanut butter sandwich. After checking out the Playboy, I dressed – with great trepidation – in something. And as I did, I found myself blaming Harold. And not for the first time, I wondered what he was doing tonight.

*(Lightchange. **DAN** exiting as **HAROLD** enters. We are in a video store.)*

HAROLD. Scorsece. Dear friend. Traffaut. Mon ami. Kirusawa.

*(A small bow of homage. And now **LINDA** enters.)*

LINDA. Hello, Harold.

HAROLD. Linda! What are you doing here?

LINDA. Oh, just movies.

HAROLD. Yeah? What'd you get?

LINDA. Cinema Paradiso, McCabe and Mrs. Miller and, for sentimental reasons, Women on the Verge of a Nervous Breakdown.

HAROLD. Wow, these are great movies. I love these movies.

LINDA. Yes, well, Janet and I aren't sure what we're in the mood for yet. Whatever goes best with dry Chablis and Chinese.

HAROLD. Chinese?

LINDA. Mmm. Setzuan beef, chicken with walnuts and cold sesame noodles. We always get too much but then we like to eat it for breakfast. So what movie are you getting?

HAROLD. Me? Oh, uh…

*(And **ANDREA** suddenly enters.)*

ANDREA. Harold, look! It is too in! Pretty Woman! I'll check it out!

*(then; to **LINDA**:)*

Hi!

*(And she hurries past them. **HAROLD** is silent.)*

LINDA. *(dryly)* Have a nice evening, Harold.

*(**LINDA** exits. **HAROLD** looks like he wants to cry.)*

HAROLD. Robert Altman…and cold sesame noodles.

*(He turns and exits. Lightchange. Offstage we hear a loud rock band with a female vocalist. Up-stage people enter and begin dancing and bobbing to music. They're at the entrance to a club and are queuing up to get in. **DAN** now forces out of the throng and moves downstage, trying to get away from the noise. He is wearing a combination of his and Dan Jr.'s clothes – baggy jeans, a t-shirt – and a tweed jacket.)*

DAN. *(loud; to the audience)* They're not the Stones, are they?

*(The abruptly music ends and **DAN** applauds along with everyone else.)*

DAN. *(cont.)* Wait a minute, wait –

*(**DAN** takes earplugs out of his ears.)*

There. You know, I remembering seeing the Stones on Ed Sullivan for the very first time. I was, what, eight maybe? My father was younger than I am right now.

(a beat)

Jesus, how the hell old does that make Mick Jagger?

*(**CHARLOTTE** enters. She is wearing a t-shirt and jeans.)*

CHARLOTTE. There you are! I thought I saw you out in the audience.

DAN. Hi! Sorry, I was late. I had an accident on the way here.

CHARLOTTE. With your car?

DAN. No, with my clothes.

CHARLOTTE. Look at you, you look great.

DAN. So do you. And one of us is not lying.

CHARLOTTE. I am so glad you made it.

DAN. I am too. You were something else up there.

CHARLOTTE. No.

DAN. Yes. You were. Even with feedback.

CHARLOTTE. What we'd really like to do is tour someday. For the experience if nothing else. That would be so cool.

DAN. You should then.

CHARLOTTE. Do you really think so? Because I want your advice.

DAN JR. You do?

CHARLOTTE. Yes. You're a successful man with a lot of life experience and I respect what you have to say.

(Everyone on stage freezes as:)

DAN. *(to the audience)* I was so used to dealing with my own children, I didn't know how to respond to that.

(then:)

CHARLOTTE. So what shall we do? You want to get some coffee or a drink? Or some food?

DAN. Only if it's on me this time.

CHARLOTTE. Or we could go back to my place.

DAN. …we could do that.

CHARLOTTE. Cool! Come on.

(She grabs his hand and spins him. Lightchange.)

CHARLOTTE. What do you want to drink? I have some red wine and there's a beer in the fridge. And I also have some 25 year-old single-malt Scotch.

DAN. Really.

CHARLOTTE. It started as an affectation. Now it's a weakness.

DAN. A glass of wine would be fine.

CHARLOTTE. Cool. Here…we go. Excuse the glasses.

DAN. No, strawberry jam jars are my favorite.

CHARLOTTE. Cheers.

DAN. *(cough)* – good year.

CHARLOTTE. I think there's still enamel left on your teeth.

DAN. It's the garage band of wine.

(looking around)

Interesting place.

CHARLOTTE. It's the Robert De Niro in Heat look.

DAN. …heat.

CHARLOTTE. Heat? The movie? De Niro plays this really cool character who says you should never get attached to anything you can't walk out the door on and leave within 30 seconds. Of course, he's a criminal. But it's my opinion that people in their 20s should live with criminal intent. Or at least pretend to. I'm joking.

DAN. Oh. Cool.

(a moment)

CHARLOTTE. I think it's only fair to warn you. I find you very attractive.

DAN. I find that very surprising.

CHARLOTTE. *(touching his temple)* I like the salt and pepper.

DAN. I season it before I go out.

CHARLOTTE. And these little lines right here.

DAN. Gifts from my children. They're your age –

(She touches a finger to his lips, shutting him up.)

CHARLOTTE. Dan. You don't have to be nervous.

(She puts down her glass.)

DAN. Charlotte, wait, stop. I think it's only fair to warn you, I haven't been with a woman other than my wife in over 25 years.

(She takes his wine glass.)

I haven't so much as kissed another women in, well, your life time. I haven't –

(She kisses him.)

CHARLOTTE. Not so difficult, is it?

(She takes his hand and leads him offstage. Lightchange as he stops, dropping her hand, coming back.)

DAN. It wasn't difficult at all. It was Christmas. It was home runs in the ninth. It was winning the lottery, that's what it was. Twice.

*(**CHARLOTTE** re-enters, a blanket around her. She stands in front of **DAN**, leaning back against him. He puts his arms around her waist.)*

DAN. I am going to ask you a question, which you do not have to answer.

CHARLOTTE. Ready.

DAN. Have you ever slept with a guy my age before?

CHARLOTTE. Yes.

DAN. Oh.

CHARLOTTE. But it wasn't like this.

DAN. This was…okay?

CHARLOTTE. What do *you* think?

(She settles back against him, content.)

DAN. What was it you – liked best?

CHARLOTTE. I like the way you looked at me. I liked the way you touched me. I like it that I feel very, very safe with you. You know, you used to come to all the high school football games? You never watched the games, you always watched Rebecca. We used to laugh about it. But I thought it was so great. That anyone could love someone so much.

DAN. Your father didn't come to the games?

CHARLOTTE. My folks were divorced when I was a little kid. I haven't seen my father in ages.

(And now, she says what **DAN** *is thinking.)*

I'm sure that's why I'm so totally and completely fixated on you.

(She kisses him. She exits. Then:)

DAN. Okay, yeah, I was a little taken back by that. Still, all in all –

*(Woooow! Music. James Brown doing "I Feel Good." **DAN** breaking into an impromptu dance to it.)*

(doing Elvis)

Thank you. Thank you very much. Okay, shoot me. I had just slept with a beautiful, 25 year-old girl! I felt elated. I felt misgivings. I wondered what she'd now expect of me. I wondered when I'd get to do it again, which, when you get right down to it, is exactly what I'd felt when I was 25 years old.

(then:)

Call it retribution but when I got home that next morning, my house was being emptied of furniture.

*(Lightchange. **DAN** turns. Two men enter and pass him, one carrying a couch.)*

Hey! What are you doing? Stop! That's my – wait!

*(They exit. **LINDA** enters.)*

LINDA. Dan? Is that you? It is you. Hi! I tried calling. You didn't answer.

DAN. Linda, what are you're doing, what's going on here?

LINDA. I came by to pick up my furniture.

DAN. What are you talking about, your furniture?

LINDA. Don't you remember? We agreed I could take my favorite pieces once I had room. Well, I do now.

DAN. But – that was over a year ago.

LINDA. Oh, there was a time limit?

DAN. No, but…

LINDA. So now you can go out and buy new things.

(abruptly:)

What are you wearing?

DAN. What?

LINDA. Those aren't your clothes.

DAN JR. Yes, they are.

LINDA. They are not. Dan. You're just getting home, aren't you?

DAN. No!

LINDA. You went out last night, didn't you? Oh, Dan. Did you get lucky?

DAN. None of your business. And I don't want new things. I like these things.

LINDA. Oh, Dan, you do not. You just don't like change. So, come on, who's the lucky girl?

DAN JR. Linda…

LINDA. Dan. We're not married anymore. You're allowed.

DAN. Linda, couldn't I at least keep the couch?

LINDA. Oh, stop. You had a fit when I bought that couch.

DAN. That was years ago. I'm used to it now.

LINDA. Well, you'll have to get unused to it. Now whatever you do, don't consider redecorating without the help of a professional. You know, you might even consider moving? This place is way too big for one person.

(then:)

Go get'm, Tiger.

(She exits. A phone rings. **JULIA** *enters from opposite sides of the stage as:)*

DAN. Yes, hello?

JULIA. *(on a cell phone)* Oh, thank goodness – Dan, it's Julia. I was just on my way home from the grocery store and a car hit a dog. The bastards didn't stop and I think it's leg is broken.

DAN. Does it have a tag?

JULIA. No. The poor thing's thin and ragged and smells like he's been eating from trash cans for weeks.

DAN. Where are you?

JULIA. Muirlands and Scenic.

DAN. Okay, I'll be right there. Oh – and don't touch him. Sometimes when an animal is injured or frightened, it bites.

JULIA. Dan, please. He's already in my car.

*(**DAN** and **JULIA** exit. Lightchange. **DAN JR.** and **SARA** enter. **DAN JR.** has a sketchpad in hand.)*

SARA. I was thinking it might go over there.

DAN JR. Yeah…I can see it. Redwood posts there, there and there…beams or slats every two feet, for the vines. You could put plantings there. Cool. Was this your idea?

SARA. And Tom's. In fact, we should probably wait and check with him. He has such a…vision of this.

DAN JR. What time's his plane get in?

SARA. I'm not sure. He missed his plane out New York last night. He was going to get an early flight. If you don't want to wait…

DAN JR. No. Tell you what. I'll do some drawings, we'll have something on paper when he gets here.

SARA. All right…

(A phone rings.)

SARA. Excuse me.

(She moves away. **TOM** *enters.)*

TOM. Hi, it's me.

SARA. Where are you?

TOM. Still in New York. The car was late and then we hit a traffic jam on the way to the airport.

SARA. Are you getting a later plane?

TOM. Nah, I have to be back Tuesday, it seems pointless. I lucked into some tickets to a Broadway show. Something, I don't know.

(sound of a woman's giggle behind him)

So, look, I'll be at the hotel and I'll call you tonight.

SARA. Fine.

TOM. Love you.

(He exits. **SARA** *moves back towards* **DAN JR.***)*

DAN JR. What do you think, something like this?

SARA. That's it exactly.

DAN JR. It's a really good idea. So…as soon as Mr. Houghton gets here, we'll show it to him and I'll get out of your hair.

SARA. I wouldn't wait. That was him on the phone. He's still in New York.

DAN JR. Oh.

SARA. He missed his plane – *again* – and he has to be back there Tuesday so it really it makes no sense for him to…to…

(And turning away, she begins to cry.)

Shit! It's just…it's all shit.

DAN JR. This is about that phone call, isn't it.

(She nods.)

I'm sorry.

(He takes her in his arms. They stand there, not moving. And we suddenly see it in both of them – the physical awareness of one another. The two of them now looking at one another. They kiss. Arms around one another, they exit.)

(Lightchange. DAN and JULIA entering. DAN wears a white lab coat and carries x-rays.)

JULIA. Will he be all right?

DAN. *(Examining the X-rays)* Well…the good news is there are no internal injuries. Breaks here and here. Lucky this one didn't puncture the lung. The leg's pretty bad. We'll just have to see.

(then:)

You know, Julia, a lot of people wouldn't have stopped.

JULIA. Of course they would.

DAN. They didn't, you did.

(then:)

You probably shouldn't wait. This might take a while.

JULIA. Dan. Would it be all right if I helped?

DAN. …yeah, sure. Come on.

(Lightchange. The sound of laughter. Lights to DAN JR. and SARA. They are in bed together. They are leafing through an old high school yearbook.)

SARA. – And here we have – taa-daa! Guess which one's me.

DAN JR. Uh…this fat one with the glasses?

SARA. No, no, no! This is me.

DAN JR. Wow. You were a babe.

SARA. Yes, I was, definitely, I was a real babe.

(She turns the page.)

SARA. Tom. He was a babe too.

DAN JR. Guys can't be babes.

SARA. Oh, you have no idea. You, you're a babe.

DAN JR. Come on.

SARA. You are. You should be illegal. As a matter of fact, you probably are.

(turning the page)

My sister, Connie. She was a year younger than me. She and her husband live in Seattle, four beautiful kids.

(She flips a few more pages.)

DAN JR. What about you, how come you never had kids?

SARA. When we were younger, we decided to wait. We had our careers, we liked to travel. And then finally we did try and nothing happened. So we tried harder. It was almost funny. Once Tom got stuck in traffic with a sperm sample that had to be at the hospital by a certain time and he abandoned the car and flagged down a cop who took him to the rest of the way on his motorcycle. And he made it. But it didn't work and so mostly it was sad. We waited too long.

(She kisses him; goes back to the yearbook. And now **DAN JR.** *sort of moves against her.)*

DAN JR. Uhm…

SARA. Oh, you are kidding. Again?

DAN JR. If you don't want to…

SARA. Oh, I want to. Believe me – I want to.

(They kiss. Lights to **DAN** *and* **JULIA** *as they enter,* **DAN** *is pulling off surgical gloves.)*

DAN. It's a little early to tell but I think he's going to be all right.

JULIA. What'll happen to him?

DAN. He's obviously a stray. When he's better, I'll hand him over to the shelter. They'll try and find him a home.

JULIA. And if they can't?

DAN. They'll put him to sleep.

JULIA. I want him.

DAN. Are you sure? He's a big dog.

JULIA. He needs me.

DAN. He's yours then.

JULIA. *(suddenly wincing)* Oh, shit, Dan.

DAN. What.

JULIA. My groceries have been sitting in the car for the last three hours.

DAN. Perishables?

JULIA. Let's put it this way – what are you doing for dinner? Because I now have several breasts of chicken that are very thawed.

DAN. You've got to be very careful how you defrost poultry, Julia.

JULIA. Dan, you can't cook water. Now come along. I'll make you pesto.

DAN. I love pesto.

JULIA. I *know*.

(Lightchange. **DAN** *turns to the audience, taking off his lab coat.)*

DAN. And so I went home and I showered and I changed. And it never occurred to me that my hair wasn't right or that my clothes weren't stylish enough. It just was.

*(***JULIA** *enters carrying two crystal glasses of wine. She touches them together to produce a bell-like tone, then hands one to* **DAN**.*)*

JULIA. Here we are.

DAN. Thank you.

(He sips. He murmurs his approval.)

JULIA. It's small winery up near Santa Barbara. Friends of mine own it.

DAN. We've all had some good times here, haven't we?

JULIA. We have.

DAN. *(looking around)* I've always liked this place – how it look, how it feels – what you've done with it.

JULIA. It's what I do. Speaking of which, I understand your house is a little empty.

DAN. Mmm, Linda left me a chair, a card table and an antique set of golf clubs. Actually it's not so bad.

JULIA. I swear, Dan, if it wasn't for women, all men would be living on beach furniture.

(A shared smile. Then, swirling his wine:)

DAN. You know, Linda used to wonder why you and I never got together.

JULIA. *(seemingly surprised)* Really? Why?

DAN. We had so much in common. We seemed compatible. I thought you were sexy.

JULIA. You did not.

DAN. You are.

JULIA. So what did you tell her?

DAN. That we were friends. Had been as long as I could remember.

JULIA. I would never want anything to change that.

(a moment)

Well – I'll get the pasta water on and a salad going and we'll be ready.

(She turns away.)

DAN. Like everything she did, Julia was a brilliant cook. And afterwards we sat in front of a fire, with coffee and desert, the easy conversation continuing. The evening went by too fast.

(He turns to look at JULIA. The sound of an antique grandfather clock tolling out ten o'clock. JULIA turning back –)

JULIA. Is it that late?

DAN. Times flies.

(then:)

Are you happy, Julia?

JULIA. Of course, why do you ask?

DAN. I just wondered.

JULIA. I choose to be happy, it's as simple as that. Are you happy?

DAN. I'm getting there.

JULIA. I think so too. Dan…

(The clock tolls again.)

Whoa, I better get going.

DAN. Oh, and listen, the dog. Call around the middle of next week. He should be well enough to take home by then. If you still want him.

JULIA. I do. And by the way, I haven't given up yet. I'm still going to find you someone.

DAN. You know, I should have mentioned something? I'm sort of seeing someone.

JULIA. Oh....that's wonderful. I want to meet her.

DAN. It's nothing serious – yet – but you will.

(**JULIA** *turns away.*)

Hey, Julia. You think maybe you could come by sometime and take a look at the house, make some suggestions?

JULIA. It's what I do.

DAN. I'd expect to pay for it.

JULIA. That makes two of us.

DAN. We'll do that then.

JULIA. Good night, Dan.

DAN. Night.

(*She exits. Lightchange.* **DAN** *turns thoughtfully.*)
I don't why but suddenly, for the life of me, I felt… guilty.

(**CHARLOTTE** *enters.*)

CHARLOTTE. Hey there, handsome. Where you been?

DAN. Hey, what are you doing here?

CHARLOTTE. Waiting for you. And now you're going to think I'm one of those Glen Close – Fatal Attraction types, standing at your window in their underwear, knife in hand, hair in face.

DAN. No. Hardly. But you should have called.

CHARLOTTE. Then you might have said you were busy.

(*She hands him a brown paper bag.*)

DAN. What's this?

CHARLOTTE. A six pack a beer. You seem like a Heineken kind of guy to me. So invite me in, I'll help you drink it.

DAN. You can come in but it's a little late for me to drink beer.

CHARLOTTE. That's okay. I hate beer.

(*She kisses him. Lights to black.*)

ACT II

*(Lights up on **DAN** and the company. They address the audience.)*

DAN. The room is soft light and shadow. I lie in bed under a sheet, watching Charlotte. She stands nude at the window, staring out at the moon. Harold is right. Just looking at her is a religious experience.

CHARLOTTE. I see him staring at me again and I have to smile. It's a compliment in a way. It's like he can't believe it. Well, that makes two of us.

JULIA. He calls and invites me over one afternoon and shows me his empty living room. He's not sure but he seems to think a couch might help.

TOM. I'm in the living room, watching television. Sara is in the kitchen. I think. I don't know what she's doing. I haven't for along time now.

SARA. I slip out the front door. It's dark out. I race across the front lawn and into –

DAN JR. – my arms. She kisses me. We collapse onto the grass.

SARA. I've been looking forward to this –

DAN JR. – to you –

SARA. – all day.

TOM. I'm watching a Seinfeld re-run when I suddenly remember something. I get up…and I go downstairs into the basement and turn on the water sprinklers.

*(The sound of lawn sprinklers. **DAN JR.** And **SARA** react as they're soaked. Turning away as…)*

LINDA. I could never admit it, not even to myself, but I've always known what I was. And it terrified me. With Dan it was so easy to pretend. We had this lovely home, these beautiful children, we were the perfect family. But. There was always an unspoken part of me that Dan could never touch. A sad place. Sad for him, sad for me.

HAROLD. We're at a party downtown. Quite the doo. Lot of successful older guys, lot of trophy wives and girl-friends. I talk with the guys about the usual – the economy, the middle east, the Cubs. I go out on to the patio and join Andrea and the other hood ornaments of God. They're having a fascinating conversation about Botox injections and Gianni Versace. The bacon wrapped scallops are good.

ANDREA. If our relationship can survive all the things he thinks I know nothing about, it can survive anything. Somewhere along the line he's decided he's supposed to be my teacher. Well! I can teach him a thing or two.

HAROLD. I'm standing at the buffet table sneaking a coco-nut shrimp when she comes up to me, grabs my arm and drags me down the hall to the bathroom. She locks the bathroom door, unzips my pants and – I think I wrenched my back.

JULIA. I'm in the middle of the Times crossword when he calls and do I want to go an estate sale. I do, fine, and so we go. At my recommendation he buys a very nice side table. He seems hesitant. A little nervous. I'm not sure if it's me or the act of acquiring a worthwhile pos-session. He seems overwhelmed by both.

SARA. I'm not sure what bothers me more. The lies –

TOM. Hey, where you been?

SARA. The movies.

TOM. Any good?

SARA. Not really.

TOM. They never are.

SARA. – or the fact that he believes them so readily.

TOM. I'm in First as always. Automatic up-grade. The mixed nuts, the free movie. The petite filet. The flight atten-dant refills my wine glass and smiles at me – one of the real ones and not for the first time. And in that moment I think…I just want this plane to fly on. And on. And on.

(a beat; calling out)

TOM. I'm in New York on Monday!

BECKY. We never knew what it was. It was dismissed as "the blues" or "Mom being moody." She finally asked for a trial separation – some time "to find herself." Dad agreed, assuming she'd come back. I think Mom did too. But then, according to her, she fell in love. At her age. I guess coming back was no longer an option.

DAN. Julia comes to pick up the dog. Food and rest and a bath have done wonders. She kneels and the dog rushes to her, licking her face. It knows who its savior is.

JULIA. He makes himself right at home. He's underfoot constantly, eats like a horse and never says thank you. I name him Roger after Anne's ex-husband. She tells me that unlike Roger, he wags his tail, whenever he sees her.

DAN JR. I get up this one morning and I head down the hall to the bathroom. I'm half-asleep, right? And I get there, only the door is locked. Only it's never locked. And then the door opens and this girl comes out. And she is, like, wearing nothing but one of my Dad's old button down collared shirts. And, like, she smiles –

CHARLOTTE. Hi.

DAN JR. – and then she heads down the hall and goes in his room. Dad. Whoa.

*(Lightchange. People exiting as **CHARLOTTE** – in one of **DAN**'s shirts – picks up some record albums up out of box, turns and –)*

CHARLOTTE. Look at these! These are so great!

DAN. You like them?

CHARLOTTE. Are you kidding? These are the best! Jimi Hendrix! Janis Joplin! The Doors! These are timeless! These are classic! These are better now than they ever were!

DAN. They're yours.

CHARLOTTE. What?

DAN. They've just been sitting in the attic, gathering dust. They're yours. If you want them.

CHARLOTTE. Want them? I mean – I'd love them, I mean – I have no way to play them.

(**DAN** *laughs.*)

CHARLOTTE. What's so funny?

DAN. You're right, you don't. I don't.

(*And now they both laugh, realizing:*)

Some gift. I don't even know if they make turntables anymore.

CHARLOTTE. They do but who can afford them.

DAN. Tell you what, forget the records, I'll buy you the CD's.

CHARLOTTE. You would, wouldn't you.

DAN. Sure. Why not? Or the turntable if you want.

CHARLOTTE. You don't have to buy me things, Dan. That's not what I want from you. I want these.

DAN. Even if you can't play them?

CHARLOTTE. I'll find a way.

(**DAN** *kisses her.*)

CHARLOTTE. And on that note, I better get dressed.

DAN. I was thinking of getting you undressed.

CHARLOTTE. Can't. I have a rehearsal. But I'll be back.

(*She exits with the box of records. Lightchange.*)

DAN. What can I say? Every time she looked at me, I felt it right down to my – uhm – *toes*. But it was more than that.

(*a beat*)

Towards the end of our marriage, Linda and I, knowing we were losing one another, decided to go a marriage counselor. Linda had been unhappy for quite some time and nothing seemed to make it better.

(Lights up on **LINDA** *as:)*

LINDA. What is it we love about each other?

DAN. Needless to say, I had a pretty long and available list. I loved her humor –

LINDA. – my optimism –

DAN. The way –

LINDA. – until recently –

DAN. – nothing ever seemed to phase her. I loved her. Linda's answer though, surprised me.

LINDA. I love the way Dan loves me. I love the way he refuses not to.

DAN. Frankly, I was hurt.

LINDA. Oh, Dan. Why?

DAN. Because it was as if you couldn't come up with anything better. What about my humor, what about my intelligence and sex appeal? Wasn't all that at least worth a mention?

LINDA. It was a given.

DAN. Linda. It felt as if you were trying to say…you don't love *me* anymore.

(She tries to speak. She can't. **LINDA** *exits.)*

Some doors, you open, you can't close them again. But! With time, I've come to realize that Linda's was not a wrong answer. To say you love the way someone loves you is to say – I love the way you make me feel about me. I love what I see in your eyes when you look at me. And that's what I felt with Charlotte. I loved what I saw in her eyes when she looked at me.

(Lightchange. A doorbell. **JULIA** *enters carrying a small sidetable.)*

Coming!

JULIA. Hi!

DAN. Julia, hi…

JULIA. I brought you your table.

DAN. My what?

JULIA. From the estate sale. I probably should have called but my moving guys were available for just a couple of hours and I thought you'd like it

DAN. …Yeah, thanks.

JULIA. You know, I was thinking about it for here in the entry way but don't you think it might look really nice in the upstairs hallway?

DAN. *(glancing off)* Uh…no, I think here is…just fine.

JULIA. Now, listen, I also brought along a couple of big pieces from the shop. You are under no obligations. I want you to live with them, see if you like them. I'll have my people bring them in.

DAN. Wait. Julia – maybe now's not the best time. I'm just getting ready to go out.

JULIA. It'll just take a moment.

DAN. Yeah, but – maybe it's best I don't get attached to things until I'm ready to buy them.

JULIA. I see. Do you still want the side table, Dan? Because I can return it.

DAN. No. Of course I want it. And I'll come by the store and see the other things.

JULIA. I should have called.

(And she starts to turn away as –)

CHARLOTTE. *(entering)* Hey. I didn't know we had visitors. Wow. Great table.

(to JULIA)

Hi!

JULIA. Hello.

(They both look expectantly at DAN.)

DAN. Julia, this is my friend, Charlotte. Charlotte, this is my friend, Julia. Julia's helping me furnish the house.

CHARLOTTE. *(all smiles)* Really? I kinda like it the way it is.

JULIA. Really? What is it you like?

CHARLOTTE. I would say it has a sort of Zen-like simplicity.

JULIA. Really. I would say it has a sort of dorm-like simplicity.

CHARLOTTE. (Good, that's good.) Well, listen, I have to run. Thanks for a great night. Oh – and some kids are getting together for a barbecue this evening. You want to join us?

DAN. Why don't we talk about that later.

CHARLOTTE. No problem.

(kissing him)

Call me. We'll pick up where we left off. Nice to meet you – Julia, is it?

JULIA. Yes. And you.

*(**CHARLOTTE** exits.)*

JULIA. That's the someone you're "sort of seeing"?

DAN. She works for the IRS.

JULIA. Does she?

DAN. But she sings nights.

JULIA. Multi-talented. You know, you're right? I don't think this is the best time for furniture.

DAN. Julia, wait! I really do appreciate you coming by.

JULIA. It's nice to be appreciated. Have fun barbecuing with the "kids."

*(She exits. **DAN** looks perplexed.)*

DAN. *(to the audience)* All right, what did I do that was so wrong here!?

*(Lightchange. **HAROLD** and **LINDA** enter.)*

LINDA. Oh, for God's sakes, Dan. Do you really think any middle aged woman is going to be impressed you're dating a teenager?

HAROLD. Why not? I was.

LINDA. Harold, I don't have to be nice to you anymore –

(hitting him)

– shut up.

HAROLD. Ow.

LINDA. I mean, really, what is it about middle aged men, they get divorced, they feel they've been given a free hall pass to throw their aging libidos at women half their age?

DAN. Throw. Do you throw?

HAROLD. Well – not throw.

*(as **LINDA** hits him again)*

Ow.

LINDA. What's really upsetting, is that by dating girls you both are re-enforcing the American cultural stereo-type that says the only value women have in our society is their sexual attractiveness. Something I would rather not pass on to our daughter, Dan.

HAROLD. Oh, come on, Linda, what are we supposed to want? Everywhere we look it's this half naked parade of youthful female flesh. It's lips and breasts and bottoms going take me, take me now, before you shrivel up and die!

LINDA. Shrivel. Are you talking about your brain or your penis, Harold.

(She hits him again.)

HAROLD. Ah! All right, you know what else? Younger women aren't as complicated as older women. They haven't been pissed off the way older women have. They like men.

(backing away before he can be hit)

Dan? Jump in.

DAN. Okay. As a vet, I might point out the male animal is biologically encoded to desire a female that is at her peek childbearing years.

HAROLD. There, you see? It's propagation of the species. For the male animal, perfectly natural.

LINDA. So is licking your balls. Enough. Andrea? Andrea, would you please come over here?

*(**ANDREA** enters.)*

LINDA. All right, sweetheart, tell me something. Before Harold, you had a history of dating older men. What do you get out of it?

ANDREA. Well. I have expensive tastes and no job skills. Mostly I was in it for the dinners, the gifts and the money.

LINDA. Yes – and?

ANDREA. Exclusively dating older men gave me social status as well as financial and emotional security.

LINDA. And?

ANDREA. I have unresolved sexual issues with my father.

LINDA. Thank you, dear. Run off and play now.

> (**ANDREA** *smiles and exits.* **LINDA** *turns and gives* **DAN** *and* **HAROLD** *a smug, triumphant look.*)

HAROLD. You really know how to hurt a guy, Linda.

LINDA. Why thank you, Harold.

> (*to* **DAN**)

I *hope* you were paying attention.

> (**LINDA** *and* **HAROLD** *exiting as –*)

DAN. Oh, come on, Linda, this is Julia we're talking about! And just because a young woman gets involved with an older man, it doesn't necessarily mean she has issues with her father!

> (*as* **REBECCA** *enters and says:*)

REBECCA. Dad, I'm involved with an older man. Dad, did you hear what I said? Daddy?

DAN. …how old?

REBECCA. Oh, god. Ancient. Early forties at least.

DAN. Is he married?

REBECCA. Oh, Daddy, I'm not that stupid. I feel like such a cliché as it is. He's divorced. And he's balding and he dresses like he's either crazy or colorblind and he has all the social grace of a robot. And if I even so much as let him hold my hand he's so grateful, it's ridiculous.

> (*her voice softening*)

REBECCA. *(cont.)* But he's a brilliant doctor. And he's funny and wonderful with children...they love him...

(She's going to start crying.)

He wants to marry me. Daddy, I don't know what do to do. This is not what I planned on!

DAN. And he's...how old?

(to the audience)

It's all I could think of to say.

(As REBECCA *furiously exits,* DAN JR. *enters. Seeing* DAN, *he starts to turn away −)*

Dan?

DAN JR. Hi, Dad.

DAN. Where you been all day?

DAN JR. Some guys and I took the mountain bikes up to Big Bear, did the lift lines.

DAN. Your bike's in the garage, Dan, I saw it this morning.

DAN JR. Uh – yeah, I used someone else's.

DAN. Oh. Well, your sister's upstairs, asleep.

DAN JR. Yeah, I saw her car.

DAN. She needed to chat a little bit.

DAN JR. Who better than with you, Dad. Can I go now?

DAN. Dan, we haven't spent a lot of time together this summer, have we?

DAN JR. No. What's your point, Dad?

DAN. Is there anything you need to chat about?

DAN JR. As a matter of fact – yeah. Yeah, I really, really do. Dad?

DAN. Yes, Dan?

DAN JR. I'm not going to college in the fall.

(He turns and exits. DAN *turns and stares at the audience, speechless. Shaking his head,* DAN *exits. Light-change. We hear the sound of* HAROLD *and* ANDREA *making love.* HAROLD *gives the impression he's holding on for dear life.)*

ANDREA. Yes – yes – yes – yes! Oh – oh – oh – oh! Ah – ah – ah – ah!

(abruptly)

Harold. What's wrong.

(a beat)

ANDREA. Harold!

HAROLD. Andrea!

> *(**ANDREA** angrily enters, a sheet wrapped around her. **HAROLD** enters behind her, a blanket around him.)*

HAROLD. Andrea – Andrea, wait! Andrea – will you wait? All I said was couldn't we do this quietly for a change? What's wrong with quiet?

ANDREA. I thought you liked it when I expressed my passion for you.

HAROLD. I do, it's just…

ANDREA. What?

HAROLD. Every night you express your passion for me. And every night I'm supposed to express my passion back to you. In multiple positions! Frankly, I'm starting to feel a little pressure here.

ANDREA. Harold, it negatively affects my self-image when you don't respond to me sexually.

HAROLD. Yeah, well, it negatively affects mine when I have to respond 24 hours a day, 7 days a week.

ANDREA. "Have to"? You "have to"?

HAROLD. No! No, I mean – all I'm saying is that sometimes – not often – I'm not in the mood for gymnastics. As a matter of fact, sometimes I'm not in the mood for sex at all! I mean, wouldn't it be nice if we could just hold each other and talk every now and then?

ANDREA. Fine. I'm listening. Talk.

> *(A moment. Another moment. And we see it in **HAROLD**'s face – the growing realization that he has absolutely nothing to say to her. And we see it in her face – she knows it.)*

ANDREA. *(cont.)* All right, I'll talk. You lied to me, Harold! You lied! You go to bed at eight o'clock! You get up at five! Half the time you don't even make it to bed, you fall asleep on the couch and you snore and shiver and fart like an old dog! I have to set a bomb under you to get you to go out at night and when we do, it's with your stupid friends because you don't like my friends anymore. You don't like what I read, you don't like what I eat and you don't like what I think or say about anything! You just pretended to, Harold, to get into my pants, which is so much bullshit. Well, guess what? I don't like what you read, Harold. I don't like what you eat and I don't like what you have to say. As a matter of fact, right at this moment, I don't particularly like you!

(She turns and exits.)

HAROLD. Andrea! We could try again! Honey-baby – !?

*(**HAROLD** follows. lightchange as **DAN** and **JULIA** enter. We sense that they are at another estate sale, browsing.)*

JULIA. Hmmm. No.

(another piece)

And this is fake.

DAN. What exactly are we looking for?

JULIA. I have no idea. But we'll know it when we see it.

DAN. I'd still like a couch.

JULIA. Dan. A couch is the least of your worries.

(stopping)

Now this is a nice piece.

DAN. How much?

JULIA. Too much. Let's keep looking.

DAN. Did I mention Dan no longer wants to go East to college?

JULIA. Really, why?

DAN. He said and I quote, "He's really getting off on contracting work." This from a kid who needs a backhoe to get out of bed weekday mornings.

JULIA. He has a girlfriend.

DAN. He hasn't mentioned it.

JULIA. Trust me. When you're 18, leaving someone to go away to college can be the greatest tragedy of your life.

(a moment)

DAN. Was it?

JULIA. Hmm? Was what?

DAN. The greatest tragedy of your life?

JULIA. Yes. It was.

DAN. Did I know him?

JULIA. …No.

DAN. Did he know?

JULIA. He was oblivious.

DAN. He must have been crazy.

JULIA. How's the youngster?

DAN JR. She's…fine.

JULIA. Must be exhausting.

DAN. Meaning…?

JULIA. I'm sure she must keep you up to all hours.

DAN. May we change the subject?

JULIA. Of course. I don't see anything here.

DAN. I kind of liked that couch.

JULIA. Dan. What time do you have to be home?

DAN. Any time. Why?

JULIA. I have a couple of new pieces in the shop. You might like to take a look.

DAN. Why don't we stop by on the way back?

JULIA. All right.

DAN. Shall we pick up a bottle of wine?

JULIA. We could do that.

(They exit. We hear the sound of a doorbell and **CHARLOTTE** *enters.)*

CHARLOTTE. Hello? Dan? Anybody home? Hello?

(And now **REBECCA** *enters. They stare at one another in surprise.)*

REBECCA. ...Charlotte?

CHARLOTTE. Rebecca, hi...I'm sorry, I didn't mean to just barge in.

REBECCA. What are you doing here?

CHARLOTTE. Is, uh...Dan around?

REBECCA. No, he went out. Why?

CHARLOTTE. Oh, uh, well...look, has he mentioned me to you?

REBECCA. Should he have?

CHARLOTTE. ...Maybe he should tell you.

REBECCA. Tell me what?

CHARLOTTE. Okay. Beck? Dan and I have been seeing one another.

*(***REBECCA*** just stares at her.)*

I mean, I know it sounds weird but it's not, it's great. He is. He's the most loving and giving man I've ever met.

REBECCA. Now I know you're kidding me.

CHARLOTTE. No. He's wonderful. And it's about time he got involved in a serious relationship, don't you think?

REBECCA. Well, someday maybe, but...

CHARLOTTE. He's really worried about what you'll think, Beck.

REBECCA. He is.

CHARLOTTE. You sound surprised.

REBECCA. No, it's just – he's never cared what I thought about anything.

CHARLOTTE. How can you say that? He adores you, he talks about you constantly. It would mean so much to him – and me – if you'd support this.

REBECCA. Charlotte, you want to know the truth, I have my own problems. But if you want to come in and wait for him...

CHARLOTTE. I would. Thanks.

REBECCA. How'd you two even meet?

CHARLOTTE. Serendipity. I work for the IRS and he was audited.

REBECCA. Now I know you're not serious.

CHARLOTTE. It wasn't his fault. He had an incompetent accountant. I guess your mother had done all the returns in the past.

REBECCA. Returns? What are you talking about? My brother has never made three thousand dollars his entire life.

CHARLOTTE. Your brother? I'm not talking about your brother.

REBECCA. You said Dan, what other Dan is there? My father –

(Silence. Then:)

REBECCA. You are seeing Dan my father!?

CHARLOTTE. Yes.

REBECCA. You and my father are – ?

CHARLOTTE. Do I detect a problem here?

REBECCA. No. No problem. Make yourself right at home.

*(**REBECCA** quickly exits. Lightchange. **DAN** enters. He's carrying a lamp.)*

DAN. Hi!

CHARLOTTE. Where have you been?

DAN. Shopping. I bought a lamp, see? What are you doing, have you been here awhile?

CHARLOTTE. Oh, only about two hours.

DAN. Charlotte, you never call.

CHARLOTTE. You were supposed to call me, remember?

DAN. And I was going to. I'm running a little late, that's all.

CHARLOTTE. Hey, decorating's a bitch. Sorry to interrupt your day.

(She starts past him.)

DAN. Charlotte, wait, hey, what's the matter?

CHARLOTTE. What do you think's the matter? I guess I'm fine to sleep with but when it comes to spending quality time together it's obvious there are other people you'd rather be with than me.

DAN. Wait a minute, are you talking about Julia?

CHARLOTTE. No, I'm talking about the weather man.

DAN. Well, you're wrong.

CHARLOTTE. Oh, am I? Am I really?

DAN. Charlotte – she's an old friend.

CHARLOTTE. Dan, friends don't just happen to stop by with furniture. Gee, and I thought I was impressive, showing up with a six pack. I'll tell you what, you ask her how she feels about you. Ask her if she thinks you're just friends.

DAN. I'm not going to insult her by doing that.

CHARLOTTE. Than ask me how I feel. Go ahead. I'm in love with you, all right? And that means I want to be the one you go shopping with. I want to be the one who goes – hey, nice chair. Maybe it's a lousy chair, maybe I'm stupid – the point is, you have to want me along for the entire ride – because I'm not interested in a short, side trip.

(then:)

Why am I even doing this? I have never chased after anyone in my entire life. Forget it, Dan, just forget it.

(She starts to exit.)

DAN. Charlotte, wait. Will you wait?

CHARLOTTE. No.

DAN. Charlotte!

(She waits; fighting tears.)

DAN. I'm the one who's stupid. I wasn't thinking. And I was being selfish. You're not a sidetrip. Please don't go. Come in?

CHARLOTTE. I better not. Someone wasn't too thrilled to see me.

DAN. What do you mean?

CHARLOTTE. Just – call me okay?

(She exits. DAN looking puzzled, then suddenly realizing:)

DAN. Oh, my God – Rebecca.

(turning)

Rebecca!?

(Lightchange. REBECCA enters, carrying her overnight bag.)

I wanted to tell you, Beck, I was going to tell you.

REBECCA. When? At the wedding? Gee, maybe Uncle Harold can be your best man.

DAN. Rebecca, no one's getting married.

REBECCA. No, of course not. Then you couldn't play the rest of the field.

DAN. Play the field? Now you're being silly.

REBECCA. I came to you for advice, Daddy. I might as well have gone to Rome for an unbiased opinion of Catholicism. Remind me to bring some friends home next time. You can date them as well. Or better yet, we could trade. Maybe you have some friends I could sleep with.

DAN. Can we just sit down and talk about things for a change?

REBECCA. Why? Why should I believe anything you have to say? Why should I believe anyone period? I have a mother who decides after 25 years of happy marriage, she's a dyke –

DAN. That's not fair –

REBECCA. A father who thinks he's Hugh Hefner –

DAN. And that is worse –

REBECCA. A brother who...who....

DAN. What. What about your brother?

REBECCA. You'll find out soon enough. And I thought L.A. was insane. Remind me the next time I get nostalgic, not to come home for Christmas.

(She exits. DAN looks up.)

DAN. Dan? Dan, are you upstairs? Dan!?

DAN JR. *(Offstage)* Dad!?

DAN. Dan, would you come down here, please?

DAN JR. *(off)* Just – hold on a sec!

SARA. *(off)* You said, he wasn't going to be home.

DAN JR. *(off)* He wasn't, he was going shopping.

SARA. *(off)* What was I thinking –

DAN. Dan!

(DAN JR., shirtless, enters.)

DAN JR. Hi, Dad.

DAN. What are you doing?

DAN JR. Nothing.

DAN. Dan, do you have someone upstairs?

DAN JR. No. Course not.

DAN. I heard voices.

DAN JR. Must have been the TV.

DAN. Don't lie to me, Dan, it wasn't the TV. Now I thought we had an agreement, no girls in the house when I'm not here.

DAN JR. There are no girls in this house, Dad.

DAN. *(a moment; calling off)* Whoever you are, please, don't make me come upstairs.

(SARA enters. She sighs, disgusted with herself.)

SARA. Hello, Dan. Haven't seen you since the wedding.

DAN. Jesus Christ, Dan.

(to SARA)

Jesus Christ!

SARA. It's not like he was completely disobeying you. I don't quite qualify as a girl, do I.

DAN. Do you think this is funny?

SARA. No. No, I'm sorry, I don't.

DAN. Does Tom know?

SARA. Of course not.

DAN. Does anyone?

SARA. We've been very discreet.

DAN. Until today.

SARA. We fell asleep, I'm sorry.

DAN JR. It was my fault, Dad. It's just that I'm so crazy about her.

DAN. Dan, you're a kid.

DAN JR. No, I'm not, Dad. I'm not.

SARA. I can vouch for that.

DAN. Don't.

DAN JR. I mean, what's really bugging you here? Is it the age thing? It's less than with you and Charlotte.

DAN. Charlotte and I are not the same thing.

DAN JR. Why? Because I'm the one who's younger? Because she's the woman? Well, I think that's hypocritical bullshit, Dad.

DAN. That's not the reason, Dan.

DAN JR. What is then? She's beautiful, she's sexy, she's smart.

SARA. He's very easily impressed.

DAN JR. What is wrong with me being in love with her? What?

DAN. Tell him.

SARA. I'm married, Dan.

(to herself)

I'm married…

*(**SARA** exits. Then **DAN JR.** exits. Lightchange as **HAROLD** enters.)*

HAROLD. So what'ja tell him?

DAN. I didn't know what to tell him.

HAROLD. What'ja tell her?

DAN. Who, Sara?

HAROLD. Rebecca.

DAN. What am I supposed to tell either of them?

HAROLD. You might start by mentioning to Rebecca that by the time she's forty, he'll be impotent, incontinent or dead.

DAN. Thanks, I'll hold on to that one. You think it up yourself?

HAROLD. No, Andrea did. We've been fighting.

DAN. Want to talk about it?

HAROLD. What's to talk about? Other than the fact that I'm tired, hungry all the time and desperate for decent conversation, things are peachy.

DAN. I'm glad you don't want to talk about it.

HAROLD. Lately I've been thinking a lot about MiMi.

DAN. How is MiMi?

HAROLD. She's dating her psychiatrist. MiMi had a Doctorate in Political Science. She kept the house clean, did the shopping, cooked the meals, she raised two kids, she taught 9 hours a week out at State on the side and when I rolled over onto her in the middle of the night, she was warm, comfortable, she fit and she liked it. I left that, Dan. Why?

DAN. Because you – and Mimi – both of you – were unhappy.

HAROLD. Exactly. And you know why we were unhappy? We got too comfortable, Dan. There were no thrills. Or surprises. There was nothing to learn anymore. There's got to be thrills, Dan. There's got to be.

(**HAROLD** *exits. Lightchange. The sound of a doorbell.* **JULIA** *enters.*)

JULIA. Hey. What are you doing here?

DAN. Can I come in for a minute?

JULIA. Sure.

DAN. I haven't caught you at a bad time, have I?

JULIA. No, I was just going through some catalogues. Come on in and sit down. Can I get you anything?

DAN. No, I'm fine.

JULIA. Dan, is everything all right?

DAN. Not really. Julia, a funny thing happened the other day – well not funny but – Charlotte and I were talking – arguing actually – and it turns out she's jealous. Of you.

JULIA. Me?

DAN. Yeah. Silly but – you and I've been spending all this time together – decorating – and she's convinced you're more than just a friend. Or rather – she thinks I'm more than just a friend to you.

JULIA. I see.

DAN. I told her she was wrong, but – I don't think she believes it. So, I thought that maybe you and I could take a little time off – just till I know where I'm going with this. You understand. Julia?

*(**JULIA** has turned away.)*

JULIA. Dan, do you remember when I told you that going away to college was the greatest tragedy of my life?

DAN. Yeah.

JULIA. You asked who it was I left behind. It was you, Dan.

DAN. …Me?

JULIA. It's always been you.

DAN. *(realizing everything)* Oh, my – oh, God, Julia…

JULIA. I know. I never could say anything. We were friends. We'd grown up together. And so I went away. And by the time I came home, you'd met Linda.

DAN. Julia, I didn't know.

JULIA. Of course not, I didn't want you to. But I must admit, I thought when you and Linda…it might finally be different. Too late, again. I hope you'll be very happy with her, Dan. I mean that. And I think that uses up all the generosity of spirit I'm capable of right now. You can let yourself out, if you don't mind.

(She exits. Light change. **LINDA** *enters.)*

DAN. You knew?

LINDA. The only person who didn't know was you.

DAN. Why didn't you tell me?

LINDA. When should I have done that, Dan? Before the honeymoon or after the divorce?

DAN. But – you two were always – close.

LINDA. She made a point of it. I think it was her way of staying close to you.

DAN. I'm so stupid.

LINDA. You have your moments.

DAN. How many times I must have hurt her…

LINDA. I'm sure you did.

DAN. I never meant to.

LINDA. Of course you didn't. You know, maybe it's naive, Dan, but the only way I've been able to go on at times, is by believing that the world is filled with decent, understanding people. Sometimes they're clueless and hurtful and they make mistakes. But that doesn't necessarily make them bad people, does it.

DAN. Is that what you think I'm doing, making a mistake?

LINDA. Why go for a used car when you can get a new one fresh off the lot?

DAN. Linda.

LINDA. I can't say you're making a mistake, Dan. Only you know that. In the end, it's about love, isn't it.

(She exits. Lightchange.)

DAN. I drove home. And I had dinner with Charlotte and we laughed and smiled as she talked about a million things. And we made love that night and we held each other afterwards; Charlotte falling sweetly asleep in my arms. And except for the little moments that intruded

– Julia's voice, her face as she left the room, I felt I had made the right decision. Hadn't I?

(a beat)

DAN. Is it me or do we all get to a point in our lives where we are just not certain about love any more? We question love. We're afraid of love. We don't trust love. We remember all the times love has disappointed us and embarrassed us. We know how easy it is for love to turn into other things. I mean – there are roads. Aren't there? A lot of them. And in the middle of the night, when you're alone – or not, which can be even worse – the ones you don't take – those are the ones you think about. And you are so afraid of making a mistake.

(Lightchange. The sound of a hospital paging system.)

Okay, yes, I was uncertain. But I didn't think I'd made a mistake. With Charlotte, how could I? But I was sure someone else was. And so with that in mind, the next day I drove to Los Angeles to save my little girl from a fate worse than death – a man old enough to be her father.

(Lightchange. The sound of a hospital paging system. REBECCA, in a doctor's lab coat, enters. She is reading a patient report.)

And then it hit me. My little girl wasn't a little girl anymore.

(She looks up and sees him. He approaches.)

REBECCA. What are you doing here?

DAN. I just felt like driving up. I wanted to talk to you.

REBECCA. I'm awfully busy.

DAN. It won't take long. How about a cup of coffee?

REBECCA. Daddy…what is it?

DAN. Rebecca, you came to me for advice a couple of weeks ago and I didn't give you any.

REBECCA. Your reaction spoke volumes.

DAN. You situation struck a little close to home, Beck.

REBECCA. Obviously. So what did you come to tell me? Do what I say and not what I do?

DAN. Rebecca, you judge people. You've done it your whole life and if you're not careful you're going to wind up alone.

(Angry tears spring to REBECCA*'s eyes.)*

REBECCA. At least I let you know how I feel about things. I don't know what you feel or think about anything anymore.

DAN. I think – feel – that the world is filled with decent people – people trying to do the best they can. Sometimes they make mistakes. In fact, when it comes to loving each other, they make a lot of mistakes. But that doesn't make them bad people, Beck. And that includes your mother who has been hurt and punished by the way you've treated her long enough.

REBECCA. How do you forgive her, Daddy, how can you just forgive her when your entire marriage was such a sham?

DAN. It hasn't been easy. But it wasn't a sham. There was nothing your mom wanted more than us, Beck – you, me and Dan. She wanted it so much she spent half her life trying to be something she wasn't. She couldn't anymore. Does that mean she didn't love me? No. Does that mean I didn't love her. I did. I still do. Enough that I want her to be happy. That's one of the things it's about, Beck – caring about someone enough you want them to be happy, even if you're not.

*(*REBECCA *is silent.)*

This man who wants you to marry him. You told me how old he is. You know what you didn't tell me? How you feel about him.

REBECCA. What do you mean?

DAN. Come on, honey. Can you talk to one another? Do you like the same movies, the same books? Is the sex any good?

REBECCA. Daddy.

DAN. Do you laugh at the same jokes, do you want the same things? If he wasn't in your life, would it hurt? Would you miss him, would you be able to replace him? Because how old or young or fat or thin or straight or gay you are, has nothing to do with that. It's all about loving someone, sweetheart. It's about the love. And that's what I think.

REBECCA. I think, Daddy…that, yes…I am in love with this man too.

DAN. Than you have your answer.

(They hug. **DAN** *kisses her forehead. She turns and starts to exit. She looks back. Then exits.)*

It isn't what I would have wished for her. But how could I tell her no?

*(***DAN*** exits.)*

(Lights up on **SARA.** *She is sitting on the floor, holding something. She has been both laughing and crying at the same time…she looks down again at what's in her hands. She clutches it to her heart.* **DAN JR.** *enters. We sense this is a memory – something that happened in the last few days.)*

DAN JR. Will you marry me?

SARA. No.

DAN JR. Will you wait for me?

SARA. No.

DAN JR. I love you.

SARA. No, you don't.

DAN JR. I do. I'll always love you. Always.

*(***DAN JR.*** exits.)*

TOM HOUGHTON. *(off)* Hey, Sara? I'm home. What's for dinner? Sara?

*(***TOM HOUGHTON*** enters. He is home from a business trip. He puts down his suitcase.)*

TOM. What the hell are you doing on the floor.

SARA. *(happily; through her tears)* Nothing. Just sitting.

TOM. What's that?

SARA. This? It's a pregnancy test.

TOM. A what?

SARA. A pregnancy test. I'm pregnant, Tom.

TOM. Uh, correct me if I'm wrong here but – you and I – we haven't…

SARA. No kidding.

(Sad laughter. Giddy tears. Then, rising:)

I think you and I need to talk.

(Lightchange. DAN enters to watch SARA and TOM exit. Then:)

DAN. *(to the audience)* Almost over.

(Lightchange. The sound of laughter. Delighted screams. DAN smiles.)

When I got to Charlotte's house that night after driving back from Los Angeles, she was on the front lawn playing tag with a group of the neighborhood's kids.

(Voices – "You're it! You're it!")

It was hard to say who was enjoying the game more, Charlotte or the children.

(A moment. DAN raises a hand in greeting. CHARLOTTE enters, breathless.)

CHARLOTTE. Hi! You wanna play?

DAN. Looks like a rough crowd to me.

CHARLOTTE. Those are my guys.

(calling off)

And this is my guy!

(We hear children's voices – "Bye, Charlotte! Bye!")

DAN. How was your day? Did you put anyone away for 20 years?

CHARLOTTE. Uh – actually no. Actually I – I quit my job today.

DAN. What? You're kidding. Why?

CHARLOTTE. Well – this is really sudden but – the band, they want to do this tour thing. And Cliff, our bass player has come into a little family money and everyone thinks the time is now. And well, I agree with them.

DAN. Well, great, yeah. I mean – it's what you wanted.

CHARLOTTE. It is. It really is. I mean, it's gonna be so great. Hey, you want a glass of wine? I went out and got some good stuff. Not to mention two very nice wine glasses. I also have both the recipes and ingredients for fettuccine Alfredo, salmon in dill sauce and a spinach and mushroom quiche. That is, if you're hungry. See? I can be taught.

DAN. Charlotte, what about us?

(*a moment*)

CHARLOTTE. Dan…you are the most wonderful man…

DAN. …You're breaking up with me, aren't you….

CHARLOTTE. I hadn't really planned to – not tonight but – yes.

DAN. I don't understand. You said you…you…

CHARLOTTE. Oh, Dan. I do. I do love you. But Dan…I can't help but feel my whole life is sort of in front of me, you know? See, I've been thinking about this a whole lot over the last few days and I think – as much as I want to – if I stayed with you, and let's say we got married or something, what if ten or fifteen years from now, I started looking at all the things I'd given up – like, the opportunities, or, like, the friends –

DAN. Children?

CHARLOTTE. I'm not ready yet but I know I will be someday. Will you?

DAN. Been there, done that.

CHARLOTTE. See? I knew that. And what if that time came and we got to that place and I started, you know, blaming you for it. I don't want to ever feel that about you, Dan, never you.

DAN. No, of course not. You're right. You have places to visit I have no interest in going back to.

(a moment)

CHARLOTTE. Dan. We can still have tonight.

DAN. You know…as much as I want to…I don't think I can do that. I think that would take something away from the nights we have had. Which I will never forget. I'm going to miss you.

CHARLOTTE. Oh, god – I hope I'm not making a terrible mistake.

(They embrace.)

DAN. You're not.

CHARLOTTE. Thank you.

DAN. No. Thank you.

CHARLOTTE. Dan? That woman? Julia? She really likes you.

(CHARLOTTE exits. DAN stands a moment. Light-change. The last boarding call is being announced for a flight to Washington D.C. LINDA and REBECCA enter with DAN JR.)

DAN JR. Well, I guess I better get on board. Mom?

LINDA. You call me when you get to D.C.

DAN JR. See ya, Beck.

REBECCA. See you at Thanksgiving.

DAN JR. *(kissing her cheek)* Just don't let Dad make the turkey. Dad.

DAN. Son. Sure you want to make this trip all by yourself?

DAN JR. The trip is easy. This is the hard part.

(DAN hugs him.)

DAN. You take care.

(DAN JR. picks up his knapsack. He turns and walks across the stage. He turns and looks back. A grin and a wave. And then he's gone.)

LINDA. Well. I have got to do something or I'm just going to dissolve into a puddle of goo.

REBECCA. Would you like to go shopping?

LINDA. *(surprised)* Yes. Yes, I'd love to.

REBECCA. And we could have lunch.

LINDA. Yes. Yes, of course we could! Uh – Dan?

DAN. You two go. I think I'll watch the plane take off and then head home.

LINDA. Come over and see Janet and me if you get lonely.

DAN. Count on it.

LINDA. *(exiting)* Now I want to hear all about Walter.

REBECCA. Aw, Mom, he is so great...

(They exit. The sound of a plane taking off overhead. **DAN** *watching it go.)*

DAN. And then *he* was gone too. The little boy who I'd carried on my back, the little boy I'd played catch with in the back yard, the little boy who'd come running down the walk to leap into my arms when I got home at night.

(A child's voice faintly – "Daddy, Daddy!")

Gone.

(A moment. **DAN** *turns.* **SARA** *has entered.)*

SARA. Hello, Dan. I was sitting over there, I saw you all come in. I didn't want to intrude. Actually, I did, I wanted to intrude very, very much but I showed a little restraint. This time.

DAN. Are you going somewhere?

SARA. Yeah. Seattle.

DAN. Business?

SARA. No, my sister's there. I plan on staying awhile. Tom and I are getting a divorce.

DAN. He found out?

SARA. I told him. But it's not about that. That was just a symptom, certainly not the cause. It's going to be lonely for you now, isn't it.

DAN. Yes. Yes, it is.

SARA. Me too. For a little while.

(*a boarding announcement*)

That's me. Dan…

DAN. Yes?

SARA. (*hesitating; then:*) Maybe I'll be in touch.

(*She exits. Lightchange.*)

DAN. There was one last thing to do. I'd been putting if off because at first I wasn't ready and then I still wasn't sure I was ready. But I had to try.

(*Lightchange. We hear the sound of an electronic bell as* **DAN** *"enters"* **JULIA**'s *antique shop.* **JULIA** *enters.*)

JULIA. I'm sorry, we're closed for the – day…

(*She stops.*)

DAN. Hello, Julia.

JULIA. Dan.

DAN. I was driving past and I saw you through the window and I thought I'd come in and say hello.

JULIA. I've been working in the back all afternoon.

DAN. Yeah, well, I drove past yesterday. It took me awhile to find a parking place.

JULIA. Rumor has it you're no longer seeing the young girl-friend.

DAN. Yeah, it's been about a month now.

JULIA. So what does that make me, the first alternate?

DAN. I'm sorry you feel that way.

JULIA. I'm sorry, that was beneath me. You were never less than up front with me, Dan. Still, that's what this feels like. You struck out with your first choice and now you turn to me. And I'm no one's second choice.

DAN. I couldn't agree more. Julia, the minute it ended with Charlotte, I knew I'd handled things badly. And I wanted to come here. But I knew that if I came too soon, you might think that I was settling – which you do. And I didn't want that because you're right, you are no one's second choice. But I also felt if I waited too long it might be too late, that you'd find someone else or they'd find you and I'd lose any chance I had.

JULIA. To do what?

DAN. To ask you another question.

JULIA. Which is?

DAN. If I was to say I wanted our friendship to become more than just a friendship, what would you say?

JULIA. Is that what you're saying?

DAN. Yes. Yes, I am. Very much so.

JULIA. I don't know what I'd say. I don't know if I can do this, I don't know if I want to or need to, I just don't know.

DAN. All right, let me try a different approach. When's the last time you were kissed?

JULIA. Hmmm. Thirteen months ago.

DAN. *(surprised)* Really?

JULIA. I was seeing a very nice lawyer in San Francisco.

DAN. A lawyer?

JULIA. It didn't work out.

DAN. A *lawyer*?

JULIA. Yes! And guess what? He was *forty*! You know, Dan, there's a lot you don't know about me.

DAN. You're right. Still, thirteen months seems like a long time.

(He moves towards her.)

JULIA. What are you doing?

DAN. Don't worry. It's like riding a bike.

(He lightly kisses her.)

JULIA. That was like being kissed by your brother.

DAN. Or re-learning a language…

(He kisses her again.)

JULIA. That was a little better.

DAN. Or jumping into deep water –

JULIA. Oh, stop.

(She kisses him – really kisses him – a keeper that leaves both of them shocked and breathless.)

DAN. …This might work.

JULIA. We'll see, won't we.

(She exits.)

DAN. Thrills. You gotta have'm. And they can be found in the most unlikely places. So. To answer the question of the evening – yes. Most of us – or at least the people I know – do get to places in our lives where we're not certain about love any more. We've been hurt by love. We've been diminished by love. Made fools for love. But somehow we soldier on. We never learn. And why should we? The alternative – living without love – is simply no alternative at all.

(lightchange.)

DAN. Guess what? There was another wedding the following year. And guess what again? I had fun at this one.

(The company entering as:)

DAN. My daughter, Rebecca, married a good man, Walter Hogan. Her mother cried. I did too. Dan Jr. was one of the usher's again. He's doing pretty well at Georgetown.

*(**SARA** enters. She is holding a swaddled infant. **DAN JR.** moves to join them.)*

We even talked Sara into coming down from Seattle. And Dan got to meet his son for the very first time. The little guy immediately peed on him and laughed while he did it. We don't know how that's going to turn out. We're not sure what to hope for.

*(**CHARLOTTE** enters.)*

DAN. Oh – and we got a wedding present from as far off as England where Charlotte and her band are trying to crack the top ten. Charlotte's involved with Cliff, her bass player. We don't stay in touch much but then there's no reason why we should.

(**CHARLOTTE** *exits. And now all the others gather around* **DAN***, smiling and chatting with one another.*)

DAN. *(cont.)* I lied. I'm crazy about weddings. I'm crazy for any occasion that brings the people I love together. As I've gotten older and the hours now seem to pass so quickly, that's what important to me – spending time with the people I love. And if I have my way, we'll be doing all this again soon. She might not have a choice any more.

(*Everyone turns to stare. Lights up on* **JULIA***. She is holding flowers.*)

Guess who caught the bridal bouquet?

(**JULIA** *moves to join them.* **DAN** *now takes the baby from* **SARA** *and all gather around him, chatting and cooing.* **DAN** *smiles at the audience.*)

(*lights to black*)

Also by
Stephen Metcalfe...

Emily

The Incredibly Famous
Willy Rivers

Pilgrims

Sorrows and Sons

Spittin' Image

Strange Snow

Vikings

Please visit our website **samuelfrench.com** for complete descriptions and licensing information.

OTHER TITLES AVAILABLE FROM SAMUEL FRENCH

EMILY

Stephen Metcalfe

Advanced Groups

Serious Comedy / 8m., 4f (to play var. roles.) / Bare stage w/drops, wings, projections & wagons or unit set

This brilliant comedy by the author of *Strange Snow, Vikings, Sorrows and Sons* and *The Incredibly Famous Willy Rivers* dares to take a politically incorrect stance about successful women. Emily is a stockbroker who mixes it up with the boys and always comes out on top. She is as cynical and ruthless as any man in her position until she meets a caring, sensitive actor who doesn't fall for her manipulative ruses. This nice guy with no money sees the girl inside the ruthless yuppie who may or may not exist.

"Glorious ... sparkling comedy with bite to it. The title character is a gold mine of a role for an actress."
– *San Diego Tribune.*

"A real winner.... A bravura balancing act right on the edge of sentimentality, finally and triumphantly crystalline in its emotional honesty.... A triumph."
– *San Diego Union*

OTHER TITLES AVAILABLE FROM SAMUEL FRENCH

VIKINGS

Stephen Metcalfe

Full Length, Comic drama / 3m., 1f / Comb. int/ext.

This heartwarming play about a contemporary American family delighted audiences at the Manhattan Theatre Club. The Vikings are not Norsemen of old, but an American family of Danish descent who pride themselves on their strength of character. They include Grandfather Yens Larsen, who founded the family carpentry business, his son Peter, and Peter's son Gunnar. After Peter's wife dies, Peter loses interest in life. His father and his son do everything they can to help him, including trying to make a match between Peter and an old school friend of his, Betsy Simmons, who is now divorced and lonely, too.

> "A play finely threaded with warmth, pathos, humor and insight."
> – *Palm Beach Daily News*

> "Beautifully written and deeply moving."
> – *Miami Herald*

OTHER TITLES AVAILABLE FROM SAMUEL FRENCH

STRANGE SNOW

Stephen Metcalfe

Full Length, Dramatic Comedy / 2m, 1f / Int

It is 5 am. on the first day of the fishing season and Megs is determined to get his buddy up, but David has a terrible hang over that is not entirely from last night's drinking. Megs and David served together in Vietnam, and David still blames himself for the death of their pal Bobby. David lives with his sister Martha, a high school teacher who is enjoying a budding romance with the delightful Megs. Together, they endeavor to convince David he has to get past the war and get on with life.

A success Off-Broadway at the Manhattan Theatre Club, *Strange Snow* became the motion picture *Jackknife* which starred Robert DeNiro and Ed Harris.

"Metcalfe writes with a sense of humor, and an ear for idiom."
– *Village Voice*

"What recommends *Strange Snow* is its basic humanity and the credibility of its affirmation."
–*Christian Science Monitor*

Breinigsville, PA USA
27 September 2010
246172BV00005B/5/P